William Bell

William Bell is the author of *Crabbe, Metal Head, Absolutely Invincible!, Death Wind, Five Days of the Ghost* and *Forbidden City*, several of which have also been published in the United States and overseas. He taught in China for two years, and is now a high-school teacher of English and history in Orillia, Ontario.

When he isn't writing or teaching, Bell enjoys camping, jogging, cross-country skiing, going to movies, plays and musical performances, reading and studying. Although he claims to "especially like being indolent," it's hard to see where he finds the time.

Also by William Bell

Crabbe

Metal Head

Absolutely Invincible!

Death Wind

Five Days of the Ghost

FORBIDDEN CITY

William Bell

Stoddart

A GEMINI BOOK

Published in 1992 by
Stoddart Publishing Co. Limited
34 Lesmill Road
Toronto, Canada
M3B 2T6

Second printing in March 1995

Published in 1991 by
General Paperbacks

First published in 1990 by
Doubleday Canada Limited

Canadian Cataloguing in Publication Data

Bell, William, 1945–
Forbidden city

1st Stoddart ed.
ISBN 0-7736-7391-1

1. China — History — Tiananmen Square Incident,
1989 — Juvenile fiction.   I. Title

PS8553.E434F6 1992   jC813'.54   C92-095120-1
PZ7.B44Fo 1992

Cover Design: Leslie Styles
Cover Illustration: Wes Lowe

Printed and bound in the United States of America

*Although this novel is based on eyewitness accounts
of actual events, it is a work of fiction. With the exception
of public figures, characters in this story are imaginary
and any resemblance to actual persons, living or dead,
is coincidental.*

This book is dedicated
to the memory of my father,
William Bratty Bell

Acknowledgements

Thanks to John Pearce for support and encouragement in the writing of this book; to Philippa Dickinson for valuable suggestions; to Chris Thomas, Marcello Tulipano, Dawn Edmonds, Candace Nelson, and Dylan Bell for helpful ideas; to Shaun Oakey for painstaking work on copy-edit; and to Doug Woolidge for technical information about acupuncture.

Last and most of all to my beloved friend for her invaluable assistance in virtually every aspect of this book, and whom, because of the subject matter of this novel, I cannot name.

Prologue

We studied a poem in English class last spring and, believe it or not, I've been thinking about it a lot lately. It's about a young soldier-king named Ulysses who sails off to fight a long bitter war in a far away country. On his sea-journey home he gets battered off course a few times and endures many adventures. When he finally drags himself out of the waves and onto his own shores he's a lot older than he was the day he left. In more ways than one.

The thing is, he doesn't fit in anymore. His adventures have changed him so much that the island kingdom he missed so much seems like a pile of barren rock. His wife and son are strangers. His subjects don't understand him.

I know how Ulysses felt. How relieved he was at first that it was all over and he was safe. How messed up and alienated and alone he must have felt after he had been back for a while.

I'm not saying that what I've written here is like the poem. This is just what I put together from a journal I was keeping when life was pretty calm, and from the notes and tapes I made when everything began to blow apart.

Dad was pretty worried that night when I sort of went mental for a few hours. He seems to think that writing this will help me re-adjust to normal life. I don't know. Maybe he's right.

I can't help thinking about Ulysses, though. Because, at the end of the poem, he takes off. He never did fit in again.

March 29

Sometimes I wonder if my father will ever grow up.

Take the day when this all started, for instance. When I got home from school I heard his excited voice rattling out of the study, going a mile a minute, obviously not listening too closely to the person on the other end of the phone because whoever it was couldn't have gotten a word in sideways.

I wondered why he was home from work so early. There he was in the chair behind his desk, leaning back so far you'd swear he was going to go over backwards like a slap-stick comedian, with the phone wedged between his shoulder and his neck, yakking away while he tried to tear open an envelope. Probably so he could read his mail while he was talking. Then later he'd probably get what was in the mail and what was on the phone mixed up. My dad.

'Yeah,' he said breathlessly into the phone. 'Just got the assignment today. What? You bet I'm excited!'

He was, too. I could tell from his eyes that something big was going on. His eyes are bright blue, like mine, and when he's turned on to something they sort of dance. They were rockin' and rollin' today, all right.

'It could be the start of something really important over there,' he went on.

I tuned him out and looked at the mess on the floor of the study. There was a new Sony Betacam just unpacked from the carton. It looked like Dad had torn open the carton in a fit of rage. There were squares and oblongs of white styrofoam lying all over, along with clear plastic bags, twist-ties, and tons of those styrofoam bits that Dad calls plastic mouse droppings. But it was just his usual method of unpacking – rip and tear until you find what's inside.

Then my eye caught another smaller box, ripped open but not emptied. I looked inside. It was a camcorder, the kind tourists and proud mommies who want to take pictures of their kids' birthday parties buy.

You'd never believe it to look at him now, his lanky form splayed out in the chair, light brown hair in a mess, shirt wrinkled, jeans creased, but my dad is one of the top news cameramen in the country. I'm really proud of him, although I wouldn't tell him that. He works for the CBC and he's won a couple of awards, like the time he just about got killed videotaping the capture of a gang of bank robbers who had gotten stuck in traffic on the Gardiner Expressway.

Long ago I realized that it was my dad's childish – no, child*like*, he always says – personality that makes him such a great camera-man. It's his crazy risk-taking that makes his work extra special.

But sometimes I wish he'd realize that there are other things in the world than cameras and film and lenses and video cassettes.

I wonder how Dad scored a new Betacam, I thought as he chattered away into the phone. 'Right. It's been thirty years since the break, with lots of conflict in the meantime. This will be a really big story.'

His voice faded as I left the study. He had finally noticed me from behind the piles of papers, stacks of files, and collection of mouldy coffee mugs on his desk and waved, so I left the room. I knew I'd get a full rundown of the conversation – whether I wanted it or not – later on, so I went downstairs to the basement.

I flipped on the light and was struck by the stern faces of a few dozen soldiers staring at me.

They were lined up in ceremonial formation, soldiers from an ancient army. They stood erect and proud on a piece of thick plywood. I looked at them from the doorway, scanning the lines of miniature men, looking for a flaw in the deployment of the ranks, a tiny lead soldier's tunic painted the wrong colour, a bowman kneeling on the wrong knee. I knew I'd find no flaws, but I looked the soldiers over anyway.

There wasn't a whole army of course, only three dozen miniature men and one war-chariot with four horses. I had made every one of them from moulds I fashioned myself, then hand-painted each one, carefully, so as to get the detail perfect. There was six months' research and then a year's work of casting, finishing and painting. Now the display was almost ready.

This was my most ambitious project. I had been a nut about all aspects of military history for a long, long time. I had model planes hanging on threads from my bedroom ceiling. Three tanks guarded my dresser. An armoured personnel carrier defended my desk. And in the basement were stored boxes of 'tin' soldiers, along with layout plans for battles. I had done the Charge of the Light Brigade, the Battle at Frog Lake from the Riel Rebellion, the Plains of Abraham, naturally, Dien Bien Phu and more. I had won lots of trophies from exhibitions put on by hobbyists all around Ontario.

But this one was going to be the best anybody had ever done. I hoped. I got the idea from a TV show I saw about two years ago. It was some kind of documentary on Chinese history, and it concentrated on a burial site near Xi'an, an ancient capital in northwest China. The first emperor of China, Qin Shi-huang, is buried under a huge tumulus – that's a tomb hidden under a man-made mountain. The Qin dynasty was in power from 221 to 207 B.C. and Qin Shi-huang, the founder, was the emperor who built the Great Wall of China. Actually, he linked together a lot of walls that were there before he came to the throne. The Chinese still haven't opened the tumulus yet. Anyway, about a klick and a half from the tumulus a farmer was ploughing the ground one day, struggling along behind his mule or ox or whatever, and he looked down and saw the top of somebody's head. Turned out it was the head of a life-size model of a soldier made of terra-cotta clay.

But that's not the interesting part. The interesting part is that there was *a whole army* of these clay soldiers buried in three different sites. The site this farmer found had more than five hundred soldiers and six war-chariots – each with four horses. There were three phalanxes, each with an honour guard of seventy men. And the soldiers were buried standing up, in ceremonial formation, facing the tumulus. The books I read about this said the soldiers were lined up as if to protect the tumulus from desecration but I'm sure that's dead wrong. It has to be. You don't face *towards* what you're defending – any fool knows that – you face *away* from what you're defending. You face the enemy.

The more I read about these terra cotta soldiers, the more fascinated I got. Each one is made with great detail. You can make out the small squares the armour is made of, the studs that hold the squares to the backing, the folds of cloth on their scarves and long coats, even the hair on their moustaches and beards. There are officers, enlisted men (you can tell from the clothing and armour), bowmen, spear-bearers, horsemen. They all wear clunky-looking square shoes.

All that got me reading other stuff about Chinese history and wars and battles. The most famous book, and the hardest to read, was *The Art of War* by Sun Zi. Great stuff. Then I got the idea of building a display based on the Xi'an site and entering it in an exhibition. I was now way ahead of schedule. The show wasn't until the end of June.

I walked over to the display and sat down on a stool behind the display. Facing me were six men who had not been painted. I turned on my desk lamp and got to work.

But I didn't get much done. The banging of the basement door and thump of footsteps on the stairs told me my dad was finished with the telephone. The lens of a Betacam appeared in the doorway and then a phony TV-announcer voice droned, 'And here is the famed military historian, seventeen-year-old Canadian Alexander Jackson, hard at work, deep in the damp catacombs of his home in Toronto.'

My dad moved into the room slowly, the new Betacam perched on his shoulder. The lens zoomed in and out.

'Tell us, Alex,' said my father, 'how – '

'Cut it out, will you, Dad? I'm trying to concentrate.'

He lowered the Betacam. A mile-wide grin was plastered on his face. He picked up one of the unpainted soldiers, looked at it, and then stared straight into my eyes. His eyes bounced and danced.

'How would you like,' he said, barely able to contain his excitement, 'to see these famous guys close up? I mean, *really* close up. How would you like to stand on the tomb of Emperor Qin Shoo-wing – '

'Qin Shi-huang, Dad.'

'Yeah, him. How would you like to stand on his tumulus and look out on the place where these guys used to live?'

'Come on, Dad, get real. We'd have to go to – '

'Right. We'd have to go to China!'

Dad and I were sitting at the kitchen table, drinking tea. I had hastily put away my paints and he was filling me in on a meeting he had had with his boss earlier that afternoon. It was hard to follow sometimes because when he was excited he rushed around inside his own sentences, starting thoughts and leaving them unfinished as he jumped over to new ones. But what I had gathered so far was that the CBC cameraman assigned to Beijing had come home with hepatitis. That's a liver disease. He didn't want to be treated in the Chinese hospitals – 'And who can blame him?' Dad had added – so he came home and now there was a correspondent in Beijing without a cameraman.

Dad said the Russian premier, Gorbachev, was making an official visit to Beijing, the capital of China, in May. Jack, Dad's boss, wanted to send Dad to replace the sick guy. He wanted Dad to go to China soon to do a lot of background stuff. And Jack had an instinct that this story would be bigger than just the state visit. 'All good newsmen and women trust their hunches almost as much as their sources,' Dad added.

'So,' Dad finished up a long, convoluted sentence, 'Jack asked me if I wanted to go. I said yes, he issued me with a new Betacam, and I went out and picked up a little camcorder for our own use because, on the way home, after we've done our work in the Centre Kingdom –'

'The Middle Kingdom, Dad.' I knew he made goofs like that just to kid me and I hated to disappoint him by letting them go.

'Yeah, whatever. And on the way home, we can flip over to Siam – yeah, okay Xi'an, don't look at me like that – and take some footage of your pals who've been standing under all that dirt for almost two thousand years waiting for you to come and see them. What do you say?'

I could hardly believe it. China! Seven thousand years of history. I'd miss the military history exhibition this spring, but there would be another in Hamilton in the fall.

'What about school, Dad? I might lose my year if I go now.'

'Oh, yeah, I forgot about that. Well, I'll call the principal and fix it. You've got pretty good marks, right?'

'Yeah, I'm doing all right. But I'd have to miss exams. Or will we be back before school gets out?'

'Doubt it. We might be there for months.'

'Could be tense, Dad. I don't know if they'd let me go.'

'They'll have to. I'll tell them we have no choice.'

I thought for a moment. I knew I had to work this through, cover all the bases. If I left it up to my dad, he'd just pack us up and away we'd go.

'They might say I could live with Mom and finish my year. They know she lives in Toronto.'

He scowled. 'You want to live with her while I'm gone?'

'Course not, Dad,' I said hastily. 'I'm just saying that might be what the principal will say.'

'Well, I'll take care of that. Where are you going to learn the most? Sitting at a desk and doing busy work, or travelling across the world?'

'You don't have to convince *me*, Dad.'

'Leave it to me, Alex. I'll charm that principal right out of his socks. What's his name, anyway?'

'He's a she, Dad.'

'Whatever.'

And he did. I have three courses this semester. My French teacher gave me an estimated mark (a B), my computer science teacher let me do a special project that took me a week of slugging to complete to make up for the stuff I'd miss, and my history teacher, Mr. Bronowski, who likes me because I'm a history nut like him, let me go with an A as long as I keep a travel diary of my experiences and hand it in to him when I get back. I started it tonight, after Dad came home and told me all the arrangements.

'There's only one wrinkle,' he added.

'What? What?' Why is it, I thought, that things never just work out nice and neat?

'Well, Jack says the assignment might be a little longer than he expected. Apparently the guy who got hepatitis is out of commission for a while.'

'How much of a while, Dad?'

'Well, maybe a year.'

'A year! That's your idea of a little bit longer? I thought our plan was to be out of Beijing by the end of May, then go to Xi'an for a week or so, then come home. A year! No way, Dad.'

'Why don't we see how it goes? Play it by ear.'

My dad is the only person in the universe who would fly halfway around the world, stay a bit, then 'see how it goes.' Sometimes he drives me nuts. 'Play it by ear' means not having a clue what we're doing next. No plans, no schedules, just floating along. I hate that. I mean, things should be organized.

'Dad, I can't live there for a year. I just can't.'

'Okay, let's make a deal. We'll cover Gorbachev's visit, do the follow-up, then go to Xi'an. Then we'll see. If one of us wants to come home at that point, we will.'

'Okay, Dad.'

He smiled and his eyes sparkled as he pushed his long hair out of his eyes.

I felt a lot better once we had things settled. So here I am, scribbling away like crazy, hardly able to write for excitement.

Because we leave tomorrow.

三月州日一
州一日州日一

March 30–31

I could tell my dad was mega-serious about this whole China caper when he came downstairs early this morning – dawn is more like it – in a clean white shirt, neatly pressed slacks and polished shoes.

He wasn't fooling me one bit, though. I knew that a few minutes after we got to Beijing – we would be living at the Beijing Hotel – he would be back into his faded jeans and T-shirt. He always says that his body rejects formal clothing the way a healthy organism rejects invading germs, and he's probably right. Me, I like to dress up once in a while. It makes me feel good. Especially when it's a special event.

Anyway, that was this morning, and already it seems so long ago. I'm writing this on the plane. My notebook is barely lit by the little reading light above me. The ride is a little rough at times, so my handwriting, which isn't prize winning at the best of times, is jiggly. The cabin lights are out and most passengers are sleeping.

We left Toronto about ten o'clock this morning. I love to fly, especially the take-offs when you feel that terrific rush as the engines roar and slam you back into your seat and you feel the plane's acceleration, then the wicked tilt, then the floating sensation as the ground drops away.

But my dad is a big suck when it comes to planes. What he does is, he gets what he calls 'blasted'. He's got it down to a science. He pops half a Gravol to calm his jittery stomach just after he checks his bags, then half a Valium when they call the flight, then as soon as the plane is up and cruising he flags down a flight attendant and orders a double whisky. All this is really strange because he doesn't drink much at all and he's absolutely death on drugs, legal and illegal. Once he's blasted, he says, the panic leaves him, and although he never *enjoys* a flight, at least he can almost relax. But it means I have to handle the tickets and boarding passes and steer Dad around.

Anyway, we made Vancouver in five hours and a bit, changed planes after an hour and a half lay-over, and took off again. We had a boring meal of some kind of chicken and then watched an equally boring movie about a rock star who loses her voice and starts up a cosmetics company. Right now we're approximately ten hours out of Vancouver. I slept a bit, but I'm too keyed up and cramped and uncomfortable to sleep soundly.

I'm six feet right on and I have to sort of fold myself into the seats they give you in the economy section. Dad is taller than me. He's beside me in the window seat, sleeping all twisted up, like a pretzel. His head is thrown back and his mouth is open and he's snoring away as if he was in his right mind. He looks pretty silly, actually. I know that a normal seventeen year old would be a little embarrassed to be sitting beside him. I'm just being honest.

You know, we're all mega-terrified that our parents will embarrass us by saying something dumb at the wrong time or answering the door in really goofy clothes or something. I used to be like that, years ago, but not anymore.

I can't sleep so I'm writing. Just letting thoughts come into my head.

I take a lot of flak from kids because I'm interested in military history and weapons and restaging battles and stuff like that. I think I'm the only kid at my school who even knows what a blitzkrieg is. The other kids couldn't care less about war and most history teachers like to babble on about governments and constitutions and the causes and effects of wars, as if the wars themselves were chapters in history that you could skip over without changing the story.

I'm not saying I'm crazy about people getting killed and cities getting bombed, but it happens, so why ignore it? Pacifists are just simpletons as far as I'm concerned. There's nothing I like better than a war movie with lots of battle scenes, noise and smoke, explosions that shake the ground, and the wicked chatter of machine-gun fire. Or a tank battle, the tanks moving like chess pieces, like in the movie *Patton*. That's the thing. It isn't the killing and ghoulish stuff that interests me. It's the battle plans and the strategy and the weapons. It's like chess or curling or bridge – those are all games I really like.

Someone – probably Mr. Bronowski – once asked me when I started getting hot on military history, and until then I didn't realize that it started around the time Mom left home and went to live on her own. My whole world fell apart. I was only twelve and I had a hard time understanding what was going on and why. At first I thought it was my fault, but Mom and Dad – especially Dad – worked hard on convincing me it wasn't. Then I figured if it wasn't my fault she left, Dad must be to blame. Maybe she got sick of him, the way he was a fanatic about his work, or the sloppy way he dressed. Mom always looked like she just stepped off the front page of a magazine. I didn't know, but I was sure, for a couple of months at least, that I lost my mom because there was something wrong with my dad.

Then one night I woke up from a bad dream. I had been

having a lot of them around then. I padded down the upstairs hall on my way to the kitchen to get some milk. When I came opposite Dad's bedroom door I heard something strange. The door was open a crack, and I looked in. Dad was sitting on the bed in a pool of soft light from the small lamp on the dresser, holding a framed photo in both hands, staring into it. I knew the picture. It was one of Mom and Dad and me at a cottage in Haliburton when I was about seven and it usually hung on the wall beside Mom's dresser. Only her dresser wasn't there anymore.

The strange sound I had heard was Dad crying. His shoulders and head shook from the deep sobs that came from down inside him.

I watched him carefully after that, because that night was when I realized how badly hurt he was, as badly as me, and I knew that no matter whose fault it was we had to face it together. We had both lost her. And the more I thought about it, the more I knew that she left us because she wanted to, and that, no matter what her reasons were, I would never forgive her.

Anyway, I'm only saying that I think that's when I started getting interested in all this military stuff. What I liked most about reading battle plans was the feeling that there were rules and strategies and traditions and everything was clear. And when I got into building model soldiers and reconstructing battles I liked the feeling of control. I'd draw plans and try to picture the troop movements, attacks, feints, retreats, traps, all that, and I'd lose myself for hours in a world that made sense.

I kept going farther and farther back into history. That's what got me into the Chinese stuff. And now, here I am, rocketing towards China, miles up in the thin air.

April 1

When the voice announcing our descent crackled over the PA, Dad woke up and tried to stretch.

'What's up?' he mumbled.

'Buckle up, Dad, we're landing in Beijing!'

The plane floated and circled for a while and I looked out the window at a curious sight. If you fly over Toronto at night, you see millions of bright white lights, like another sky full of stars. But when I looked down at a city that was almost three times as populated, I saw only bits of weak yellowish light here and there. You'd never have guessed that a huge city was below you.

The plane bumped down hard and taxied along a rough
runway towards the terminal. We hauled ourselves out of our
seats and I lifted the aluminum Betacam case from the overhead
storage bin.

We wandered, bleary eyed and exhausted, to the baggage
room. Dad was wide awake by the time we got our bags and went
through the passport and customs check. We were slowed down a
bit because of the Betacam and the other electronic equipment
we had with us – the camcorder, a small tape recorder you could
dictate into, a portable CD player, a portable shortwave AM/FM
and a Walkman. Dad had to list them all on a piece of
official-looking paper. The customs guys wore brown uniforms
and looked as bored and sleepy as I felt. As we left the passport
check we passed by glass doors leading outside. Lots of people –
mostly men – stood on the other side of the glass holding up signs
with names on them.

'There's supposed to be someone here to meet us,' Dad said as
we inched along with the crowd.

'There, Dad, look.' I pointed to a tall thin Chinese man in a
grey sports jacket. He held up a piece of cardboard with JACKSON
printed on it. Dad and I struggled through the crowd and out
the door into a cool, dry evening and walked over to our sign
man.

'I'm Jackson,' Dad said, holding out his hand, 'Ted
Jackson.'

The man gripped my dad's hand and pumped it as if he was
trying to get an engine started.

'How do you do? Welcome you to Beijing, Mr. Jackson. I am
Xu Bing-long.'

Mr. Xu gave us a big friendly smile that was jammed with
crooked teeth. He was only a couple of inches shorter than me
and had a long face, not like the Chinese Canadians in Toronto.
Most of them are fairly short, with round faces and broad flat
noses. Mr. Xu had quite a honker on him, a sharp, hooked nose
that looked almost Arabic. His voice was high, like a little kid's
but there was a bit of grey in his brush cut, so he was probably
older than Dad.

'This is my son, Mr. Xu. Alexander.'

Mr. Xu did his pumping routine on me. He held on to my hand and said, 'Welcome you to China, Ah-rek Shan Dah' – Mr. Xu had a lot of trouble getting his tongue around my name – 'hope your stay is a happy one.' He talked English with an accent, and he said words that ended in 'r' a bit like a Britisher. Like, *cah*, for car. And *Ah-rek Shan Dah*.

'Thanks,' I mumbled, wishing he'd let go of my hand.

'We have a car,' he said, and finally released me.

We got our stuff packed into the trunk of a Nissan and climbed in, Dad and I in the back and Mr. Xu in front with the driver. We pulled out of the airport parking area onto the straightest road I've ever seen in my life. It stretched away ahead of us until the yellow lamps that lined it on either side disappeared in the distance.

Dad and Mr. Xu made small talk about the flight while I settled back in the seat. I looked at my watch. It was past one in the morning, China time, and that meant we had been travelling almost twenty-four hours. I hadn't slept more than an hour or two of that.

Dad was talking excitedly. Now that he was back on earth and not threatened with another take-off he was his old self, asking questions and barely letting Mr. Xu get an answer out before hitting him with another one.

I gathered from the conversation that Mr. Xu was assigned by the government to the CBC news team, which was made up of two people, Dad and Eddie Nowlan, and his job was to help arrange interviews, visits to factories and other places the reporters wanted to visit, interpret for them, get tickets for them if they wanted to travel, etc., etc. I wondered why Eddie Nowlan couldn't do that for himself, but I was too tired to butt in with questions the way I usually would.

After a while we entered the city and drove along wide, nearly deserted avenues. Then the Nissan made a sharp turn into a parking lot in front of a big building. The car swept through the crowded lot, turned onto a ramp that curved up to the front door, and came to a stop.

'Beijing Hotel,' announced Mr. Xu in his high voice.

I was stiff and sore and half asleep. After he had loaded himself up with our bags, Mr. Xu led me through the big glass doors, across a wide lobby, and into an elevator. Mr. Xu said something in Chinese to a sleepy woman in a hotel uniform who yawned and pushed a button – which was crazy, because it was a self-serve elevator.

The elevator stopped, and we stepped into a long, dimly lit corridor.

'This way,' said Mr. Xu, and we followed him down the hall. He stopped and knocked at a door.

It was opened by a heavy middle-aged white man. A thick-stemmed pipe jutted out from under his walrus moustache. He looked different than he did on TV, where I'd seen him a million times giving news and analyses from all over the world, and lately from China. Eddie Nowlan was one of the CBC's top news correspondents. On TV he was always Edward, but now he looked more like an Eddie in wrinkled shirt, baggy pants, and slippers.

'Hello, Lao Xu,' he boomed. 'And you must be Ted. Welcome to the middle of the Middle Kingdom.'

They shook hands as Dad said, 'Glad to meet you, Eddie. I've been looking forward to working with you.'

Eddie looked curiously at me, eyebrows raised. 'And who's this?'

Oh god, I thought, realizing that Eddie hadn't been expecting me. Dad had probably forgotten – or neglected – to mention that I was coming.

'My son, Alex,' Dad said. 'I, ah, brought him along for the experience. I thought he'd get a lot out of it.'

Eddie didn't look too pleased as he held out his hand, which felt cold as it gripped mine.

'Hi,' I managed. 'Glad to meet you.' I would have been, too, if I hadn't felt so stupid and humiliated turning up unannounced. This guy was a big name all over Canada. I had never met a celebrity before. Leave it to Dad to screw it up for me.

'Well,' Eddie growled, 'we'll try and find a spot for you.'

The suite of rooms consisted of a small vestibule with four doorways. One led to a bathroom, one to a brightly lit office, and the other two opened on to good-sized bedrooms. Eddie Nowlan led us into the office. A picture window filled the far wall and reflected the office lights back to us like a dark mirror. On the sill was a row of flower pots of different shapes and sizes with all kinds of green plants in them. In front of the window two big desks faced each other. One had a word processor and a couple of telephones. On the other was an ancient typewriter, a fax machine, a tape recorder, and piles of tapes. Both desks were stacked high with wire in- and out-baskets, paper, and newspapers.

'Take a load off,' Eddie ordered, waving towards a couch.

Dad put the Betacam on the floor. He and I sat down on the couch while Mr. Xu helped Eddie stow the suitcases somewhere. I thought I could hear Eddie grumbling to him from the other room. Eddie came back and got some bottles out of a small fridge. He snapped them open, plunked them down on the coffee table, and collected some glasses from one of the desks.

'Have to rinse these out. Be back in a minute,' he said.

'Well,' Dad said, looking around with sparkling eyes, 'I guess this is the newsroom.'

'Dad, didn't you tell him I was coming?'

'I guess it slipped my mind. Don't worry, it'll be okay. You look like you could sleep for a week,' he added, changing the subject like he always does when I'm mad at him.

Mr. Xu came in and took one of the armchairs. He crossed his legs at the ankles and settled back.

'Do you live here in the hotel, Mr. Xu?' Dad asked him.

'Oh, no. I live about twenty minutes of bicycle from here. Please call me Lao Xu,' he added. 'Lao means "old." Xu is my surname. In China we put the surname first. My given name, Bing-long, means "Bright Dragon".'

'And I hope you'll call me Ted.'

'Would you like I give you a Chinese name?' Lao Xu said, looking at me.

'Yeah! That would be great.'

'Okay, I call you Shan Da. Sounds like your name, Ah-rek Shan Dah, which is hard for Chinese to say.'

'What does it mean?'

Lao Xu got up from his chair and went to one of the desks. He wrote two characters on a piece of paper and handed it to me. The paper showed:

山大

'Shan Da means Tall Mountain in Chinese. Good name for you, as you are a tall boy.'

I folded the paper and put it in my pocket. 'Thanks,' I said. Then, 'Dad, can we go and see the Great Wall tomorrow? And the Forbidden City?'

Dad laughed. 'We'll see, we'll see. Give me a break, will you?'

Eddie came back with the clean glasses and poured beer into three of them. He dumped some orange pop into the other and handed it to me.

He raised his glass. 'Welcome to China, Jacksons, and here's to successful news gathering.'

I tried a sip of the pop. It was tasty, but very sweet.

Dad took a long swallow from his glass, then another. 'Ah,' he said. 'That tastes good. I was thirsty.'

'Yep, Beijing beer is excellent,' Eddie said, wiping foam from his moustache. 'And I ought to know, right Lao Xu?'

Lao Xu had hardly touched his beer. He laughed politely at Eddie's joke.

After a few more minutes of small talk Dad took a look at me and said, 'Alex, you'd better hit the sack.'

'I'm okay, Dad,' I said, not convincing anyone. Including myself.

'Come on. Off you go. Beijing will still be here when you get up tomorrow. Or is it already tomorrow? China is twelve hours ahead of us, right? And we crossed the international date line.'

'Right.'

Eddie led me into a large bedroom with two single beds in it. He said good night and left the room. Almost before he had shut the door I had taken off my clothes, dropped them on the floor at my feet, and crawled into the bed nearest the window. I fell asleep right away.

When I woke up, the bedroom was dim, but I could see light around the edges of the curtains. In the other bed Dad was sprawled in a tangle of twisted blankets, snoring away, one foot hanging over the edge of the bed.

I lay there, groggy and dazed, until my excitement came back with a rush, the way you feel right after a thunderclap. I was actually in China!

I pulled on my wrinkled cords and went to the bathroom and splashed water on my face. Back in the bedroom, I pulled on a T-shirt, slipped into my deck shoes, then rummaged around in my suitcase until I found my China guidebook. I left the apartment, heading for the elevators.

I went up to the roof, got off the elevator, and ran down a hallway and pushed open the door. It was chilly out, and clear. The air smelled dry, dusty, and a little smoky. I looked over the wall to the noise and bustle of Chang An Avenue seven floors below. Wow, what a sight. I have never seen a street like it. There are ten lanes, three each way for cars and buses, and two each way for the rivers of bicycles that flowed past. The riders weaved in and out, acting just like car drivers in a jam in Toronto – impatient, ringing their bells, pushing each other on as soon as the light changed. A few had passengers – they sat on the rat-trap carrier behind the driver, legs dangling inches from the pavement.

I took a walk along the roof to the west until I got to the corner. Below me, on the other side of a narrow side street, was more than six hundred years of history – the Forbidden City, where the emperors had lived from 1368 until the early 1900s when the monarchy was overthrown. It's a city in its own right, sitting quietly in the middle of modern, busy Beijing, surrounded by a high wall and a moat. Inside the thick walls are courtyards and wide, low buildings with gracefully sweeping roofs covered with orange tiles. There are even pine trees and gardens, alleys and parks.

The wall of the Forbidden City's southern border faces Chang An Avenue across a moat that's spanned by three marble bridges. In the centre of the wall is the Tian An Men, The Gate of Heavenly Peace, looking out on Tian An Men Square.

I made a promise to myself to visit the Forbidden City as soon as I could, and then I went back down to our rooms to see if Dad was awake. He wasn't. I wrote this stuff and now that I'm finished I'm tired again. So I'm going back to bed.

April 4

Tonight Eddie gave us a Chinese banquet here at the hotel to welcome us to Beijing. On the expense account, he said. Dad had on his usual scruffy outfit and Eddie looked very unglamorous in a brown tweed jacket and grey pants. Lao Xu was there, too. He's a great guy. As soon as he came to the hotel tonight I asked him to teach me everything about China, especially customs. And history.

He laughed and said, 'Okay, Shan Da, I'll try my best.'

We went to a private banquet room on the fourth floor. It was a little room, with a huge round table covered with a white cloth.

I was expecting the kind of Chinese food we got in Toronto – sweet-and-sour breaded chicken balls, barbecued pork, sweet and sour spare ribs, chow mein – stuff like that. Not here.

As soon as we sat down Eddie and Dad started talking business. Eddie may have been a celebrity but he was making a crummy first impression on me. He bossed my dad around too much, giving him instructions every five seconds, as if Dad was his assistant or something, rather than a colleague. As far as I was concerned, without my dad, Eddie was just a voice. I tried to shut out his booming voice and talk to Lao Xu.

I asked him what was on the dishes in the centre of the table. He pointed to them one at a time. 'These are called cold dishes – sausage, chicken breasts, sliced cucumber in sweet sauce, diced cucumber in hot sauce, raw chopped Chinese cabbage with dark vinegar, and dried fish.'

Great, I thought. What a thrill. Maybe the chicken will be okay.

'And what are those black things?'

'Preserved eggs. Try one.'

I tried to use my chopsticks, but after a few minutes of trying to pick up the jelly-like strips of preserved egg, I gave up and used the fork. I should have stuck to the chopsticks. The egg felt like glue in my mouth.

The waiters and waitresses started bringing in the hot courses. Each time a dish arrived the top would be removed with a flourish and the waiter would announce the name of it – in Chinese. We got deep-fried chicken, and chicken balls in oyster sauce. Two or three kinds of fish served on big oval platters – fish with the heads and tails still on and the eyes staring at you, daring you to eat. Slices of duck with crisp, fatty skin. Shrimps with hot red sauce that made my eyes water. Shredded pork with green pepper and black mushrooms. Beef bits with ginger and onions.

I tried it all and liked most of it. While we ate, Lao Xu and I talked – or he did, mostly. Turns out he's a history buff, too. He told me a few legends. Some of them were so funny I could hardly eat for laughing.

All through the meal the waiters and waitresses would keep our glasses filled. I got orange pop but the three grownups had beer, sweet red wine that Dad said tasted like syrup you'd pour on ice cream, and, in tiny glasses, wine called Mao Tai that they used for toasting everything they could think of. After the first crack at the Mao Tai stuff Dad switched to beer.

When we started eating I noticed that Lao Xu took the bones out of his mouth with his chopsticks and dropped them beside his plate. It looked pretty rude until I thought about it. There was no room on the tiny plate and, unless you liked the idea of tossing the bones onto the floor, nowhere else to put them. It wasn't long before we all had a little pile of bones in front of us, like some kind of weird sacrifice.

The only dish that really threw me was some black strips of something or other about two inches long, in a sauce. I popped one in my mouth and tried to chew it but it was like rubber without much taste.

'It's sea cucumber,' Lao Xu said. 'A delicacy.'

He went on to explain that the sea cucumber isn't a plant. It's a creature that swims – 'Like this,' – and he moved his hand in the same motion a worm or snake would make. Then I realized he meant sea *slug*.

I only had the one piece.

Just when I thought my stomach would blow up from the pressure, one of the waitresses brought in a huge platter of *jiao-zi* – fat steaming dumplings stuffed with ground pork, cabbage, ginger, garlic, and spices. They were great.

Then soup. Then ice cream. Then fruit.

By the time we finished, I could hardly get out of my chair. Eddie was wobbling from too many toasts, Dad burped every few seconds. There was tons of uneaten food on the table. I said to Lao Xu we should take it with us, like we did at home.

'No,' he answered, 'that's the Chinese way. The host must always offer much more food than the guest can eat. If there isn't more than enough food he will lose face. So, Shan Da, whenever you go to a Chinese home, when you are finished eating and can eat no more, always leave some food on your plate and some beverage in your glass. Don't empty your plate like you do in the West. Here, your host will always put something more on your plate to show his generosity.'

All that food made us sleepy. Lao Xu went home, Eddie fell into bed, Dad crashed on the couch with one of my novels, and I started writing in my journal. But I'm going to bed, too. It's about ten o'clock, and dark out. Ten in the morning in Toronto. My friends will be finishing up first class – French. I wonder if my body will ever adjust to Beijing time.

四月六日

April 6

All the history I took in school seems like a pile of dust next to what I saw today. I mean, I walked on the Great Wall of China! I was in an emperor's tomb – over five hundred years buried in the ground! The emperor, not me.

Lao Xu is amazing. The guy seems to know everything about China. He rattles off information like a computer, complete with quotations from Chinese classical literature and Chairman Mao Zedong, the man who ran China until he died in 1976. And Lao Xu makes it all interesting. When I told him I was a military history nut he told me that his father had been a soldier who fought in the Red Army when he was seventeen and died fighting the war against the Japanese. Lao Xu's father had participated in the Long March, one of the greatest feats in military history, where a hundred thousand Communists had retreated twelve thousand, five hundred klicks from Fujian Province in southern China to the west as far as Tibet, then far north to Yanan, fighting Nationalist soldiers and local war-lords almost the whole way. By the time Mao Ze-dong led them into Yanan – more than a year after the retreat had begun – there were only about ten thousand of them left.

'Many of the men who run China now, the men high up in the Communist Party, are men who were on the Long March,' Lao Xu told me. 'They are getting pretty old now, some in their eighties. But they refuse to retire.'

Lao Xu practically worships the PLA, the People's Liberation Army, which is what the Red Army has been called since Liberation in 1949. He calls them 'a true people's army' and says that whenever there is a flood or other natural disaster the PLA will be there, helping the people. They don't wear a lot of fancy ribbons and braids and stuff on their uniforms. The only way you can tell an officer is to count the number of pockets on his coat. Officers have four, enlisted men two.

By the time we got back to the hotel it was late afternoon, so Lao Xu said goodbye to me in the parking lot and went to get his bike in the bicycle parking area. There were hundreds of bikes there, and how he found his among all those Flying Pigeons and Phoenixes, almost all of them black, I don't know.

I wished in a way that his dad was still alive so I could talk to him about the Long March. What an adventure!

Dad and Eddie were sitting in the office talking when I got in.

'How's the Foreign Devil tourist?' Eddie asked around the stem of his pipe. He was watering his flowers carefully, caressing the leaves as he worked his way along the windowsill.

'Tired,' I answered as I tossed my pack onto the couch and opened the little fridge, hoping to find a bottle of orange pop there. I was beginning to like the stuff.

'Have a good day?' Dad asked. 'Get some good shots?'

I swear my dad sees the entire world through a lens. I plopped down on the couch, heaved a big sigh, and took a long drink. The sweet icy pop numbed my throat as it went down.

'Yeah, I think so, Dad. The wall was great. Fantastic. Unbelievable.'

Dad laughed. 'So, what are you saying? Did you like it or not? How about the Ping Tombs?'

'*Ming*, Dad. The tomb was okay, if you like cold dark tunnels and stairs and crowds and piles of dishes and stuff. You should have come with us.'

His blue eyes darted a look at Eddie. 'Oh, well, I was too busy. Lots to do.'

'Did Lao Xu go home?' Eddie asked, lowering himself into a chair. 'I wanted him to do something for me before he left.'

'He's gone, Eddie. Dad, does he ever know his history! He makes Mr. Bronowski look like an amateur.'

'Really?' Dad said. 'What's his background, Eddie?'

'Lao Xu? He's a Master of Arts. Went to Beijing University, I think. Wrote a few books, too.'

'Then what's he doing working for you?' I cut in, realizing after I asked that my question probably wasn't too polite.

'Because in China you don't choose where you're going to work, Alex. When Lao Xu graduated he was assigned to the Foreign Ministry. A few years ago, when China opened up to foreigners, they put him to work with correspondents because he speaks excellent English and pretty good French.'

'But that doesn't make any sense.' I thought of my school again. 'He should be teaching history.'

Eddie nodded. 'I agree. I'm sure he does, too. But things don't work that way here.'

'Why doesn't he quit this job and apply for something he wants?'

'Because you can't do that here, Alex. Chinese don't have the right to choose where they work. Even if he arranged a job teaching at a high school or university, his present work unit would only have to say no and that would be it.'

I took another swig of the pop, emptying the bottle. 'Okay, why can't he just tell them to go to – why doesn't he just leave.'

'Do you know about *hu kou*?' Eddie asked as he sat down.

I shook my head.

Dad said, 'Never heard of it.'

Eddie sat back in his armchair and relit his pipe. '*Hu kou* is a sort of census and residence card mixed together. Every family has a green residence book. Kids are in the father's book. To get your ration coupons – a lot of food here is rationed, like rice, cooking oil, meat, milk, and more – you have to show your *hu kou*. No green book, no coupons.'

'I think I'm beginning to see,' Dad said.

'Yep. If you tell your boss – your leader, they call him or her – to stick his job in his ear, and you quit and go to another job, he refuses to transfer your *hu kou*.'

'He can do that?' I asked angrily.

'Your leader has tremendous power over your life, Alex. In lots of things, not just your job. *Hu kou* is also the way the government controls population movement. For instance, if you live in the country on a farm and you want to move into the city, you can't. The Public Security Bureau won't accept your *hu kou*. So you have to stay where you are. Otherwise, millions of people would move into the cities, which are already overcrowded.'

I let all this soak in for a minute. I could see the part about the population. There were well over a billion people in China. But the stuff about the jobs sounded stupid to me.

'Anyway,' I said, 'it's too bad. Lao Xu is a terrific guy. I really like him.'

'Yeah,' Dad said, 'me too.'

Eddie smiled a cold smile. 'Yep, Lao Xu is the nicest spy you'd ever want to meet.'

'Spy?' I almost shouted. 'What do you mean?'

Eddie took a big swallow of beer and shifted in his chair. 'Well, part of Lao Xu's job is to keep his superiors up to date on our activities. As a matter of fact,' he laughed, 'if one of us sneezes, the Party boss says Bless you. Or would, if she weren't officially an atheist.'

'Come on, Eddie,' I complained. 'Stop talking in riddles.'

'Alex, you know that Lao Xu's job is to assist me and your dad as an interpreter, right?' And you know he helps us if we want to arrange an interview with someone, or dig up some background for a story. For instance, tomorrow morning we're going to the Citi building – you've seen it, it's down past the Friendship Store – to do a little piece on a new joint venture between China and another wine industry in France. Well, Lao Xu made the connections and got approval from the government to set it up.'

'Approval? Why do you need approval?'

'Because it's a government project. Remember, this is a centralized communist state. The government doesn't have to talk to the CBC about its plans to do business with French grape-growers. This isn't Canada, where the government officials are responsible to the citizens because the citizens elected them. Political power here belongs to a very few, very old men. The Chinese government can do whatever it pleases, including send us all home tomorrow if it wants. Lao Xu is also arranging for us to cover Gorbachev's visit. We'll do our interviews, write our copy, then take the tapes down to CBS or CNN and ask them nicely if we can use their satellite feed to send the video to Toronto. But that satellite feed is set up by the Chinese government especially for the state visit, and they can pull the plug anytime.

'Lao Xu wears a couple of hats, Alex. He's assigned by the Ministry of Foreign Affairs to help us. And he's good. He has lots of contacts and he gets us stuff that helps us keep ahead of a lot of the other news agencies. But part of his job is reporting back to his superiors on all our activities.'

'But what's to report? I mean, you're not doing anything wrong or illegal. What do they care?'

Eddie took another swallow of beer, then puffed furiously to get his stove going again. 'They care because we're foreigners. Foreigners are not trusted here – or in any country where there is no freedom. Number two, your dad and I are journalists from a country that has freedom of the press. We're used to writing and broadcasting and' – he nodded to my dad – 'photographing what

we want. Here, the news is managed totally. The Chinese have
cynical but true saying. In the *People's Daily* – that's the officia
Party newspaper, like *Pravda* in Russia – in the *People's Daily* onl
the date is the truth. And it's like that with all the loca
newspapers, like *Beijing Ri Bao* or *Guan Min Ri Bao*. They're all ru
by the state. Get the picture?'

I nodded slowly.

'If the Central Committee wanted, it could shut down al
foreign correspondents in a day or two. Lao Xu is the govern
ment's link to us and to what we're doing.'

I had a sinking feeling in my gut. I felt hurt and angry an
stupid. I felt betrayed. The guy who I thought really liked me
who was becoming my friend, was an informer. Was he taking m
around to tourist spots and talking to me just to get informatio
on me and my dad and Eddie for a file? And yet at the sam
time I was a little bugged at Eddie for telling me. He seemed t
enjoy it.

My mind quickly replayed my trip to the wall and the tombs.
tried to remember things Lao Xu had asked me. There wasn'
much – just stuff about school. I had done most of the asking
Then I tried to recall things I had told him. Something kep
returning to my mind. It was the way he laughed. That ironi
laugh. It was quiet and short, but you couldn't mistake it. Th
laugh said, 'This isn't the way things ought to be, but that's life.
It wasn't a spy's laugh.

But what did I know about spies?

Eddie heaved himself out of his chair. His slippers slapped a
he padded across the rug and got another beer from the fridge. H
poured some into Dad's glass before topping up his own.

'Try not to be too hard on Lao Xu, Alex,' Dad said. 'He like
you. I know he does. If he didn't, he wouldn't take you aroun
like he did today. That's not part of his job.'

As Eddie lowered himself into his chair he said, 'Maybe so. Bu
part of his job is reporting on us. You can be sure that everything
he knows about you and especially your dad is on file with th
Public Security Bureau. Each one of us has a dossier.'

He laughed cynically. 'If it makes you feel any better, someone is also reporting on *him*.'

It didn't. Maybe Lao Xu and I could still be friends, but now I knew there would always be a wall between us.

April 7

Today I felt really down. I don't know, maybe it was just jet lag or something but I got homesick. I wished I could sleep in my own water bed in my own room, listen to my tunes on the stereo in our living room, maybe have a fire going, call up my friends on the phone – and eat real food.

I only brought six novels with me and I'm into the second already. Where will I get stuff to read? And there's nothing on TV here. The only program in English that I can find is a really lame show that comes from England called *Follow Me*. It's supposed to teach English. They say things like 'Do you really have your own lorry? Smashing!' or 'Who is in the loo?' and fascinating stuff like that.

The most frustrating thing is that I can't really *do* anything because I can't speak Chinese. As soon as I step outside this boring hotel I'm isolated – totally. I can't shop or anything unless Lao Xu comes with me to translate. He's really good about that and he helps a lot, but it's kind of a pain to stand in the middle of a store getting stared at by a couple of dozen Chinese while Lao Xu and a salesperson rap on about me like I'm a total retard or I'm invisible.

In our hotel suite everybody but me has work to do. Eddie keeps giving me these I'm Busy And You're In My Way looks.

And Dad. He's in his element, buzzing around, humming to himself like he was totally demented, having a great time. This morning, when he thought I had left the suite, he said to Eddie that if it was up to him he'd live here for a year, no problem. Now I'm afraid he'll want to stay for longer. I hope he's not planning to go back on our deal. I can hang in for as long as we planned, but after that I'm out of here. Even if I have to go back alone.

April 8

I got up at around nine this morning, which is practically the middle of the day in China. I heard Dad, Eddie, and Lao Xu in the office, so I slipped into the bathroom, showered and returned to the bedroom without disturbing them. I didn't really want to talk to Lao Xu this morning. I could hear the word processor keys clicking in the background while Lao Xu yelled into the telephone, shouting '*Wei!*' every few seconds.

I went to the hotel dining room and had some toast, then I cruised the hotel shops for postcards. I got some with pictures of the wall or Forbidden City on them, plus a map of Beijing, and a copy of *Beijing, Old and New*. I was forming a plan of what I wanted to do for the next week or so to kill time.

I went and sat in the lobby coffee shop and wrote a card to Mom – Dad said I should write to her once in a while – and watched the tourists strolling by or browsing at the long glass display cases across the lobby where they sold everything from lacquer ware to stuffed pandas.

I opened the map, pleased to find that the streets were named in Pin-yin, the alphabetic system the Chinese use to teach kids how to pronounce the characters in the national language, Mandarin. Because the names of the streets and sites were written in this way, I could read them and follow the street signs, which were written in Pin-yin as well as normal Chinese characters.

I love maps. I think I got hooked on them from my interest in military history and restaging battles. I like to just sit and read them sometimes, sort of getting a picture of a city's layout in my head and imagining what strategies I'd use if I were invading or defending it. Toronto, for example, is easy. All the streets are laid out on a north-south/east-west grid, except for spots like the Don Valley or the Humber River where the course of the rivers sometimes leads to streets whose direction varies from the pattern. Beijing was the same, I saw right away. The map showed the Forbidden City pretty well in the centre with Bei Hai, a long lake, to the west of it. The map showed where the old city walls once stood. The walls and most of the gates have been torn down.

The plan I mentioned that was forming in my mind was this: I'd see if Dad would let me buy a bike so I could get around on my own. Then, with my map and copy of *Beijing, Old and New* I could tool around the city and see what I wanted. Dad and Eddie seemed to be getting busier every day, and even if they weren't I doubted Dad would want to go exploring with me. There's no way I was going to sit around in the hotel all the time.

I sat back and looked at the tourists some more. Then my eye caught something moving high in the corner where the wall met the ceiling. A video camera. I could tell from the angle that it wasn't pointed at the display cases. It was watching people in the lobby.

It made me uncomfortable to think that in some little room in the hotel someone was eye-balling us all. It really bugged me. Alex, you're getting paranoid, I said to myself. After all, I had seen them in stores in Toronto. Still, I felt exposed, examined. I guessed the feeling was just fallout from what Eddie had told me about Lao Xu. Then I remembered something Eddie had said that night that sort of went by me at the time. He said that someone is probably reporting to someone about Lao Xu. Maybe Lao Xu feels just as bad about the situation as I do.

'Well, I don't know,' Dad was saying in that tone of voice parents use when they *do* know and the answer is going to be no.

'Come on, Dad, I'll be all right. I'm not a baby, you know.'

'But what if you get lost?'

'How can I get lost? I've got a map.'

'I can help, Ted.'

Until then, Lao Xu had kept out of the discussion – that's what Dad calls an argument.

'I can write something on a card for Shan Da. If he gets lost, he can show it to a taxi driver or a bus driver, or anyone. Everyone knows where Beijing Hotel is.'

'Great,' I chimed in. 'And I'll tell you what, Dad. I'll buy a compass, too.'

Eddie looked up from his rapid-fire typing and blew out a cloud of foul-smelling smoke. 'He can even take one of the two-way radios. Most of the time they just lie around here, unused.'

I didn't really want Eddie's help, but there was no way I was going to turn it down. 'Well, how about it, Dad?'

'All right, Alex. If you promise one thing.'

'Yeah, yeah, I know. Be careful.'

'No, I know you'll be careful. I want you to put everything you see on video.'

I should have known.

After lunch Lao Xu and I set out to buy a used bike.

四月十四日

April 14

Nin hao? Nin shen ti zen me yang?

Hah! I can talk Chinese! Or at least a week's lessons worth of
Chinese, which doesn't sound like much, but the way Teacher
Huang puts it to us, we are learning a lot. I can already do a little
shopping and ask directions and buy tickets and talk about how
delighted I am to be in China and witness the Four Moderniza-
tions and great progress of the Motherland, blah, blah, blah.

About a week ago I found out there's a school for foreign
diplomats' kids near Ri Tan Park, which is a block or so north of
the Friendship Store – You Yi Shang Dian, in Chinese – and I

asked Dad if I could go and learn a little Chinese. I was getting sick and tired of feeling like I was deaf, dumb, and blind all the time, never knowing what was going on around me. And I knew the only way out of that feeling was to learn some of the language.

Dad agreed and said we'd have to find a school. We were in the office at the time, and Lao Xu said he thought he could help, and a couple of days later, most of which he seemed to spend shouting into the phone – 'Wei? Wei?' – he had found me a place. Eddie was amazed.

'I know *diplomats* who can't get into that school!' he said.

Lao Xu just smiled and said a former classmate of his was director of the school.

'Ah,' Eddie said, '*Guan xi.* That means "connections", Alex.' Then he said to my dad, 'It's a hard language to learn. I hope you're not wasting your money, Ted.'

I gave Eddie a dirty look but he didn't notice.

'Don't worry about Alex. Once he decides to do something, get out of his way.'

Eddie took his pipe out of his mouth and laughed. 'I wonder where he got that from.'

I get up at seven every morning, shower and dress and eat, hop on my Phoenix and bike along Chang An. There's usually a good stiff breeze, and because the city is so flat, I can *sail*. I unbutton my jacket and hold the bottom straight out from my body with one hand, making a sail, then just sit there and get pushed along by the wind. I got the idea from people I saw doing it.

By the way, speaking of my jacket, I don't get stared at as much when I ride along now. I got sick and tired of that, too, so one day I marched along Wang Fu Jing Street near the hotel to the big department store. I bought one of those light coats that Westerners call Mao coats, a blue hat with the red star above the peak, and a pair of those corny mirror sunglasses that a lot of young guys here think are cool. I'm glad no one back home can see me. But I'm disguised enough, with my blond hair and blue eyes covered, that I get by without the stares.

Chinese is really different from English or French. The hardest part is the tones. You can say a sound four different ways, using the tones. I can't explain it in writing, but take the sound *ma*. First tone means Mom, second means hemp or flax, third means horse, and fourth means curse or swear! As if that's not enough, if you put *ma* without a tone on the end of the sentence, it changes the sentence from a statement to a question! There's more. Chinese verbs have no tense. Adding *le* to the end of a sentence changes it all into the past tense. I don't know what you do about the future. In Chinese there's no 'he' or 'she'. Both are *ta*.

As if that isn't enough, we learn Chinese by writing the words in Pin-yin. Except some letters are pronounced differently from English. X is *Hss*, so Lao Xu sounds like *Hssoo*. Q is a hard ch sound, Zh is like our J, and Z is a sound English doesn't really have!

Enough of that. I go to school in the mornings, then head down to the Friendship Store to get a pop and a snack. In the afternoons I pack up my gear in my backpack and go out for a reconnaissance trip. I take some food, a couple of Cokes, a million battery packs, the 8mm camcorder, videotapes, my audio recorder – which I haven't used yet, but you never know – my Walkman and some rock 'n' roll tapes, and my VHF two-way radio. It's a little thing, about the size of a pack of cigarettes or a pager, with a range of five or six miles in the city and five times that in the country. It has a power-saving feature when it's on receive mode so I can leave it on while I'm out and be sure the battery won't wear down. Dad can call me anytime he wants. We use channel one.

What I did, I bought one of those bamboo baby seats a lot of people have on their bikes. It fits on the rat-trap carrier behind the seat over the rear fender. I tie the camcorder to the carrier so it points out behind me, put it on autofocus, and lock it on. I have a little box with a hole in it that covers the camcorder but allows the lens to protrude a little. When I get to a part of the city I think is interesting, or that I think Dad might find interesting, I just get off the bike, lock the camera on, remount and ride slowly along.

I tool around the streets, exploring. I've been through the

Forbidden City – which looks mostly like a ghost town, with expansive empty courtyards – and saw the Nine Dragon Wall, out to the Summer Palace, which is an hour's ride to the outside of the city past Beijing University, and to the Temple of Heaven Park. Those places were weird, in a way. One minute you're in a noisy, polluted city. Then you walk through a gate and blink your eyes and suddenly four or six hundred years disappear. You see graceful, elegant buildings with glazed roofs, wooden latticework on the windows, and quite cool interiors. Gnarled ancient pines stand in peaceful courtyards. Except on Sundays, when the places are packed with people.

The most fun I've had is hopping on my bike and exploring the parts of the city the tourists don't get to or even know about. A lot of Beijing is old residential neighbourhoods where there are *hu tongs* – alleys – instead of streets, with walls along the alleys and gates that lead into courtyards. I read that these walled neighbourhoods were designed to be easily defended in times of war. So naturally I had to check them out.

One day I took a walking tour of Tian An Men Square. Lao Xu told me I could pick up a lot of fairly recent Chinese history by visiting all the spots there, and Eddie added that if I got bored there was a Kentucky Fried Chicken place at the south end of the square.

The square is mega-huge. It's almost forty hectares, with trees lining it on the north/south sides. I wandered through the Museum of the Revolution and the Museum of Natural History. Then I walked across the sun-baked square, past the tourists and kite flyers and families and popsicle saleswomen and professional photographers, past the tall square pillar of the Monument to the People's Heroes with the gold writing on it, to the west side where the Great Hall of the People is. The PLA soldiers stationed at the doors, with their wrinkled green uniforms and green running shoes and old bolt-action rifles, didn't look too intimidating to me. I strolled past the Mao Ze-dong Memorial Hall and the two tall blockhouses that were once part of the city wall. They're called 'gates' in Chinese. Then I crossed Qian Men Lu – Front

Gate Street – which is even busier than Chang An Avenue, to the chicken place. It was too crowded.

Lately when I get back to the hotel the first thing Eddie and Dad ask is, 'Get any good footage?' After dinner I hook the camcorder up to the TV and show them what I have. Once, they liked some footage of traffic flowing past the Drum Tower in the pouring rain so much that Dad transferred it to superVHS tape to use as a lead-in to one of Eddie's reports. He sent it back to Toronto. We don't know yet whether it got on the news but Dad paid me anyway.

'A newsman ought to be paid for his work,' he said. I felt pretty good about that.

四

月

十

五

日

April 15, 12:15 A.M.

Everybody – Dad, Eddie, Lao Xu – has been busy tonight. I can hear them working in the office.

There were rumours that a Party bigwig named Hu Yao-bang is really sick and may die any time. Also that when he does there will be a big student demonstration in Tian An Men Square. Apparently Hu had lost his position in the government a couple of years ago because he had been too lenient with student demonstrators at that time. The big boss, Deng Xiao-ping dumped him. Eddie was pretty excited, puffing away like an old steam engine, and Lao Xu looked a little bit nervous.

Dad asked me to go out after dinner and do a recon of the square and draw a map that he can use to get around with his camera to photograph the demonstration. I told him I had already checked out the square and could do a map from memory. Here it is:

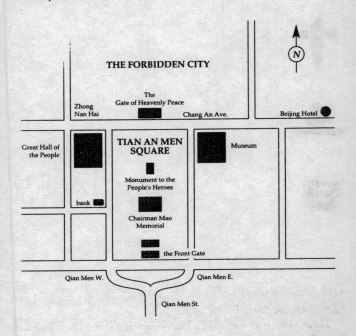

Dad is getting his equipment ready. He's humming away like an old lady almost in her right mind. He's driving me nuts. The whole apartment is alive with wires snaking along the floor, leading to our battery pack rechargers – for Dad's Betacam, the two-way radios, my camcorder, my tape recorder, and Walkman. I think we're drawing more power than the nearest factory.

Whatever happens, Terrible Teddy will be ready.

四月十五日

April 15

This morning I got out of bed and wobbled towards the bathroom in my usual morning fog. Something wasn't right, though. Then I realized what was different. There were no noises coming from the office.

I padded into the room and was practically blinded by the morning sun pouring through the windows. Squinting, I went to the windows and drew the drapes. The office was messier than usual, which meant it could have won a prize from the *Guinness Book of World Records* and Dad's equipment was missing. I scratched my head and wondered where everyone was.

44

Still not clued in to the world enough to figure out the obvious, I had a shower and returned to the bedroom. On my desk was a note.

Alex,
Hu Yao-bang has died. We're going to the square to cover the student demonstration (if it happens).

P.S. Thanks for the map.
P.P.S. Use the two-way radio if you want to contact us.
                                                                    Dad

The map was gone all right.

I went down to the dining room for breakfast. The place was like one of the Ming tombs. Waiters and waitresses stood around talking, paying no attention to the half-dozen customers. I finally had to go up to one of them to order some eggs and toast. He said the dining room was 'No open', so I talked to him in Chinese. It worked. He smiled and took my order for eggs and toast. When I got them they were half-cooked and cold.

Even though it was Saturday and school in China goes six days a week (ugh!) there was no way I was going to pass up the chance to check out the demonstration. I knew from the emptiness of the dining room that something big was happening.

I took the elevator to the roof. I had to perform the laborious task of pushing the buttons myself because the elevator person was not there. When I got to the roof I joined some tourists who had already gathered there. From where I stood I could see the museum, the northwest corner of Tian An Men Square, and most of the Great Hall of the People. The square was crowded with people.

When I got back to the office I looked down into Chang An Avenue. The sidewalks were packed tight, buses inched along the road, taxis crept past honking angrily. Cyclists were so tightly jammed together that many people had given up and were walking.

I picked up the two-way.

'Dad? This is Alex. You there? Over.'

I could hear lots of crowd noise in the background when Eddie answered. 'Alex? Eddie here. Yep, your dad and I and Lao Xu are right near the Monument to the People's Heroes. What's up? Over.'

'Nothing, Eddie. Just wondered what was happening. Over.'

'Lots, so far. The base of the monument is already piled high with flowers. The students have organized things pretty well, so that people who want to leave something on the monument in Hu's memory line up.'

Eddie's voice sounded like he was doing one of his news broadcasts. Cool and distant. 'So far everything is orderly. Your dad is trying to climb up the back of the monument's base to get a better angle for his pictures. Is he always this crazy? Over.'

I laughed. 'Most of the time. Over.'

If you want to come down, walk. You'll have trouble getting your bike through the crowds. Over.'

'Okay, Eddie. I think I will come down for a look. Maybe I'll see you. Over.'

'Bring me a cold beer, will you? Over and out.'

I loaded up my backpack with my usual electronic goodies and took the elevator down to the lobby and left the hotel.

Well, I did go to the square, but it was pretty boring. There *were* a lot of people there, but hundreds of thousands of people just means lots of people. Most of them were about university age, and many of the people near the monument and the flowers were crying. There were also a lot of cops.

But I don't know anything about Hu Yao-bang, and I'm not interested in politics anyway. I'm not a cynic like some kids I know. I don't think all politicians are crooks or anything. I just think they're boring. So I didn't stay in the square too long.

April 24

Tonight after dinner Lao Xu turned up. After saying hello to Dad and Eddie, he said to me, 'You doing anything special now, Shan Da?'

I put down my book. 'No, not really.'

'Want to come with me to hear some live history? Military history? It's nearby,' he added to my dad.

'Sure,' I answered. 'Is it okay, Dad?'

Dad nodded.

'Bring your tape recorder, Shan Da.' Lao Xu said. 'And better wear your Chinese disguise.'

A few minutes later we were cycling through a cool evening along the west side of Tian An Men Square, which was well lit up by the streetlights. There were lots of people in the square, most of them near the base of the Monument to the People's Heroes. Lots of cyclists out, too.

Once past the square we continued south along Qian Men Street, the route the emperor used to take when he went to the Temple of Heaven to pray for good harvests. There's a big park there. I read that Mao Ze-dong used the park as an execution ground to get rid of his political enemies, but I didn't say anything to Lao Xu about that. He likes Mao.

Qian Men is a narrow street with lots of *hu tongs* leading off it. The buildings along the street are very old. We turned right onto one of the *hu tongs* and Lao Xu led the way as we rode slowly, dodging carts and pedestrians and mini-transports – those big three-wheeled bikes with the platform behind the driver.

Lao Xu stopped and we pushed our bikes through a gate and into a courtyard about twice the size of a tennis court. We locked our bikes under a tree and crossed the courtyard to an old building. Inside was a darkened room, full of small round tables. A couple of dozen men sat around the tables smoking, drinking tea or beer, and talking. Some were playing Chinese chess on the paper 'boards', picking up the round pieces and slapping them down as they completed their moves.

Lao Xu and I found an empty table at the end of the room, right beside a small dais. I sat down while Lao Xu went to a sort of bar and bought a couple of bottles of orange pop and some beer.

Most of the men at the other tables kept their hats on, so I did, too. I hoped that in the dim lighting no one would see my blue eyes.

'This is a kind of teahouse, Shan Da,' Lao Xu said in a voice so low I could hardly hear him. I knew he was talking low so we couldn't be heard. Once the men heard foreign talk there'd be no end to the staring.

'In old Beijing,' Lao Xu continued, 'it was the custom for a lot of people to come to the neighbourhood teahouse and sit with their friends and talk. Not so much anymore, since most people have radio and TV. In this place they have storytellers, old men from the neighbourhood who tell tales from Chinese classical literature.'

We sat for a while and gradually the tables filled up. None of the patrons looked to be less than forty years old.

Three old guys came in and walked slowly up to the dais and stepped up. Each one carried a low stool and what I took to be some kind of musical instrument. One had a sort of guitar that Lao Xu told me was called a *pipa*. Every finger and the thumb of his left hand bore a white guitar pick. The second old man set up a little percussion set – gongs, small cymbals, and some wooden blocks.

'And that's an *erhu*,' Lao Xu said, pointing to the third man. 'Means, two strings.'

The third man had lowered himself carefully onto his stool. He held the *erhu* straight up and down, with the round part, about the size of a large pork-and-bean tin, on his thigh and the long neck, like a guitar's, only much thinner, came up to his shoulder. In his right hand he held a bow, but this bow's strings went between the *erhu* strings and the frame.

I heard some rumbling of voices near the door and I turned to see a *really* old man hobble in. He was dressed in what looked like black pajamas, with strips of cloth wrapped around his ankles to hold the cuffs tight and a wider strip of cloth around his waist for a belt. He was totally bald, bent over, and he walked as if he was afraid his bones would break from the strain.

He made it up to the little stage and sat down even more slowly and carefully than the *erhu* player. Someone put a tiny wooden table down beside the old man. Another person appeared with a white teacup with a lid on it and set it down on the table.

The storyteller sat quietly, a thin gnarled hand on each knee, and closed his eyes. After a moment he nodded once. Then the music – if you could call it that – started up. The *pipa* was sort of normal but the *erhu* sounded like a violin with stomach flu, and the percussion went *boing, boing, boing, tick, tock, clunk*. It was the strangest collection of noises I'd ever heard.

The weird sounds coming from the instruments were nothing compared to what came out of the old man's thin mouth. You'd have sworn he had put a clothespin on his nose and then tried to imitate an angry little girl with tonsilitis. His high, reedy voice soared and dipped and quavered as he slowly moved one hand through the air while the other rested on his knee. He'd change hands when his voice changed pitch.

'*Tian xia da shi, fen jiu bi he, he jiu bi fen,*' whined the old man, and from behind him came *boing, boing, crash tick, tick, tick, tock, tock.*

I didn't pay too much attention to the noises after the first few seconds because I was trying to follow Lao Xu's quiet interpretation.

'The empire, long divided, must unite,' his soft voice floated from across the table, 'long united, must divide. History teaches us this lesson.'

The story had begun.

'Day after day, week after week, the armies were encamped at the Red Cliffs of the mighty Yang-ze River. On the north bank, the endless ranks of the ambitious Cao Cao, whose greed sought to swallow down the house of Han. On the south, Sun Quan, ally of the noble Liu Bei, kinsman to the Han, who opposed Cao Cao as his oath in the peach tree garden demanded. Between them the wide swift Yang-ze River.

'Zhu Ge-liang was adviser to Liu Bei. He had come down from his retreat in a mountain monastery to help Liu Bei defeat Cao Cao. But resourceful Zhu Ge-liang had many enemies, among them one of Sun Quan's military advisers, Zhou Yu. Zhou Yu hated Zhu Ge-liang so much that he decided to kill him.'

While the cymbals clashed dramatically and the fingers of the *pipa* player and the *erhu* player raced up and down the strings, Lao Xu took a long drink of beer.

'Zhou Yu wanted to trick Zhu Ge-liang so he could cut off his head without criticism, and he thought long and hard for a plan. Finally he came up with an idea. He called Zhu Ge-liang to his quarters, welcomed him, and gave him a feast. After they had eaten and drunk, Zhou Yu began to talk of the war and the upcoming battle that would decide the fate of all.

'Zhou Yu: I highly esteem your valuable counsel, Zhu Ge-liang. Most of my experience in warfare has been on land, in the mountains. What type of weapon do you think best for river fighting?

'Zhu Ge-liang: For naval warfare, the bow and arrow are best.

'Zhou Yu: Ah, what a pity. I had wanted to attack Cao Cao soon, but I do not have sufficient arrows to wage war against the superior numbers of Cao Cao. I am certain there is no one under heaven who could supply us with enough arrows in time.

Zhou Yu waited in silence, certain that the pride of Zhu Ge-liang would speak.

'Zhu Ge-liang: I think I may be able to help, General.

'Zhou Yu: I have the highest admiration for your august self, sir, and for your prowess in war. But the Feng Shui man has advised that we must do battle within ten days, or we shall lose the war. I am certain that no one under heaven could make ten thousand arrows in ten days.

'Zhu Ge-liang: I can supply you with ten thousand arrows. He smiled, took a sip of rice wine, and spoke again: And I can do it in three days.

'Zhou Yu smiled inwardly at the rashness of Zhu Ge-liang. As he talked, he pretended to admire Zhu Ge-liang while casting doubt upon his promise. Finally Zhu Ge-liang signed an oath saying that if he didn't supply Zhou Yu with ten thousand arrows in three days, he would give Zhou Yu his head.'

I took advantage of another burst of bongs and clashes to ask Lao Xu, 'What's *feng shui?*'

Lao Xu took another swallow of beer. Interpretation is thirsty work. 'No one in those days would make any major decision, none, without first consulting a – what's the word? – a sort of astrologer who would consult his charts and interpret signs and give you the luckiest date for what you were planning to do. He was called Feng Shui Xian Sheng – Mr. Wind and Water.'

The ancient storyteller's right hand began to float in the air before his eyes as his reedy voice began again.

'On the first day, Zhu Ge-liang obtained twenty river ships, each with a crew of thirty men. Then he ordered one hundred and twenty wagon loads of straw and eighty bolts of black cloth. Zhu Ge-liang met with the crews and gave them instructions. Then he looked at the sky and shook his head and went away.

'Zhou Yu's spies reported this activity to Zhou Yu, who demanded: How many arrows has he gathered?

'The spies answered: None. He has not even called for bamboo, varnish, feathers and glue.

'Zhou Yu threw back his head and laughed and said: In two days I will have his head.

'On the second day, Zhu Ge-liang returned to his twenty ships. The crews were busy. One-third of them stretched the black cloth on the decks of the ships along the gunwales, then tied the cloth to posts to form walls. Meanwhile, two-thirds of the men were making hundreds of straw men. In the afternoon of the second day, the crew placed the straw men on the ships, lining them up behind the cloth walls that ran down the sides of the ships.

'Zhu Ge-liang looked at the sky at the end of the day's work. He shook his head and went away.

'Zhou Yu's spies reported to him again.

'Zhou Yu: How many arrows?

'None.

'Again he laughed and exulted that he would soon have Zhu Ge-liang's head.

'On the morning of the third day the fog lay on the river so thick that it was as if the sun had lost its power, and so dense that a man standing at the stern of a ship could not see the bow.

'Zhu Ge-liang was at the riverbank early. He smiled to himself. He ordered the men to tie the boats together, stem to stern, and they set out onto the broad swift Yang-ze. The twenty boats made a long line as the crew rowed upstream through the fog, towards Cao Cao's camp.

'By noon, Zhu Ge-liang's ships were opposite Cao Cao's camp. The noise and the din of the thousands upon thousands of soldiers told Zhu Ge-liang he had arrived, for even at noonday the sun did not penetrate the heavy fog. Zhu Ge-liang ordered the ships to form a line, bows to the west, sterns to the east. Then he told the crew to beat on their drums and shout to make as much noise as a navy a thousand times as strong.'

The old storyteller paused and his hand returned to his knee as the instruments made some dramatic plunks and bangs and whines. I looked around the smoky room. Every face was turned to the old man who was sitting there in old-fashioned clothes, telling a story that was written more than six hundred years ago and which described events that had taken place eleven hundred years before that. The old man sat still as a stone, looking off into nowhere. This must have been the way people were entertained in the days when almost no one could read. I was trying to decide if this was better than TV when one of those wrinkled hands rose like a bird off a thin black knee and began to move gracefully in the air.

'In the camp of Cao Cao, half-a-million strong, the soldiers heard the pounding of the drums out in the river and the clamour of voices rolling out of the fog. Quickly they sent an urgent message to Cao Cao.

'Cao Cao was wary. He thought that Sun Quan was using the fog as cover for a full attack. He gave orders. Thousands of bowmen rushed to line up along the riverbank several ranks deep with their braced longbows and metre-long arrows. The riverbank seemed to bristle with cocked arrows as the archers awaited to order to shoot.

'Soon the air sang with the twang of bowstrings and the hiss of flying arrows as rank after rank of bowmen loosed their shafts and the fog above the river rained bamboo arrows onto the ships. The arrows pierced the cloth walls, struck the straw men, and stuck there, or buried their points fast into the ships' hulls. When the ships and straw men were thick with arrows, Zhu Ge-liang ordered the crew to turn the boats around.

'As the line of boats turned in the current and took up the new position, the fog thinned enough for Cao Cao to make out the shapes of the ships. He redoubled his efforts. Out on the broad swift Yangt-ze the pounding of the drums kept up, the shouts of the crew continued, and the arrows skimmed through the fog towards those ships, seeking the enemy who were not there.

'In the late afternoon, the fog began to thin further when a breeze from the west sprang up. Zhu Ge-liang ordered the boats to withdraw downstream, but not until the whole crew shouted in unison, "Thank you for lending us your arrows, Cao Cao. You can be sure we will return them soon!"'

Boing, boing, boing, crash, crash, tick, tick, tock, tock. The old wrinkled hands returned to the thin black knees as the men at the tables around Lao Xu and me laughed and nodded, lit up fresh cigarettes and began to talk again. Most of them ignored the musicians and the storyteller as the old men left the dais and filed slowly out of the room.

I was trying to decide whether I liked that story better than the Long March and I decided that I did. I'm not sure why. Maybe simply because it was older – about 1,700 years older!

I think it was at that moment that I *really* understood how long Chinese history stretched back, and how many wars there had been. Sun Zi's *The Art of War* was written about 500 BC. The edition I had contained both Sun Zi's words and commentary by – guess who? Cao Cao, the enemy general on the story I just heard. Cao Cao had written his comments about 750 years later. And there I was in an old teahouse tonight, listening to it all.

Lao Xu cut in on my thought. 'That story gives us an expression that you will often hear in Chinese, Shan Da. *Cao chuan jie jian.* Its literal meaning is "Straw boat borrow arrows", but the idea is that you use your opponent's strengths against him.'

He sighed, 'In China, our greatest strength is the people. But so often in our history, we fight among ourselves.'

As we rode home through the chilly evening we passed Tian An Men Square. The flowers piled on and around the Monument to the People's Heroes in memory of Hu Yao-bang were still there.

So were the police.

April 26

What a tough morning in class today. Teacher Huang really went after me. I'm getting lazy with my tones, he said. It bugged me, especially since I knew he was right. I've been spending all my time looking around the city. But what the heck, I'm only learning Chinese for fun. He seems to think I want to be a diplomat.

One thing about school in China, it sure is different. And most of the differences I don't particularly like. I already wrote that school runs six days a week. There's no discussion in class and you sit in your seat for the whole morning except for a ten minute break. In the Chinese schools you have to do exercises in the break, but in our school you get the whole ten minutes for yourself. Big deal.

Teachers here are revered. No one challenges them, even on an opinion, and of course no one even *dreams* of talking back. My teacher is called Huang Lao Shi. Huang means 'yellow'. Lao Shi means 'teacher'. That's the form of address for men and women teachers. It sounds pretty funny to a Canadian. I wonder if Chinese kids have nicknames for their teachers, like Death Breath McKay, my geography teacher in grade nine. The guy could kill a crowd at one hundred metres. The Chinese government could have used him to clear out Tian An Men Square the other day.

Old Huang's okay I guess, even though he got on my case this morning, telling me my pronunciation was *bu hao*, not good.

I got home at the usual time to find Dad and Eddie working away. Which means that they were sitting in the armchairs talking and taking notes, planning stuff. Which means Eddie was giving out a lot of orders. Gorbachev's visit is coming up and all the news hounds in the city are working like mad. Sometimes I think they complicate things too much.

Shortly after lunch Lao Xu rushed in, looking nervous. He held up a newspaper and started talking really fast.

Eddie calmed him down. I stayed in the room, worried, because I thought maybe something bad had happened to him personally.

'Its the editorial in *Ren Min Ri Bao*,' Lao Xu said.

That's the People's Daily newspaper, the official mouthpiece for the Chinese Communist Party.

Eddie fired up the word processor and sat ready to take notes. He showed no interest in Lao Xu's feelings.

Dad said softly, 'Sit down, Lao Xu. Take your time. What's up?'

For such an excitable guy, Dad can be a real calmer-downer when someone is hyper. It's himself he can't control sometimes.

Lao Xu twisted the paper in his hands. While he talked, Eddie typed.

'The editorial attacks the students who demonstrated in Tian An Men Square on the fifteenth. It says that the students are – here, let me read it – "promoting chaos".'

Dad did his What's The Big Deal frown. I certainly didn't get it. Eddie kept typing, which meant that he did get it.

'I didn't see anything bad when I was there, did you, Dad?' I said.

Lao Xu answered for him. 'You couldn't read the posters and banners, Shan Da. A few of them called for more democracy and an end to corruption in the government.'

'*More* democracy!' Eddie snorted. 'You have to have *some* to have *more!*'

'I'm afraid,' Lao Xu continued, his voice anxious, 'that things will deteriorate. Please don't put that in your report, Eddie.'

'Don't worry, Lao Xu. That's conjecture anyway.'

'Why?' Dad asked. 'Forgive me, Lao Xu, but I guess it's too complicated for me.'

'Ted, I'm afraid maybe the students will get more and more militant. You know how young people can be. The government will have to get more harsh, because if there are demonstrations when the premier arrives the government will lose face.' He ran his fingers through his close-cropped hair. 'I think this editorial is a warning.'

I left the room to pack up my gear for my daily bike tour. It all seemed pretty strange to me, getting worried about a newspaper article.

One thing I thought about though as I said goodbye and left: If Lao Xu was a spy who reported on all three of us to the Party, why would he come to us and voice his fears? He was upset, I could tell that. Nobody is that good an actor. Was it all a trick? And if it was, what was the point?

April 27

Ever seen a million people before? All in one place, I mean? And on a hot sunny day? Well, I have. I saw them today in Tian An Men Square. It was a scary sight, I'll tell you. And awesome. A million heads of black hair. Two million brown eyes.

When I left for school Chang An Avenue was more crowded than usual, but when I got back after lunch – I had a big hamburger at the Jian Guo Hotel – the avenue was practically clogged.

I put together my pack of electronic goodies. I found Dad's note in the usual place, on my desk. It said that according to the news on TV this morning, there were already fifty thousand students in the square protesting against yesterday's editorial, the one that Lao Xu had been worried about. Apparently it made the student organizers angry to be called 'elements of chaos', whatever that's supposed to mean. Anyway, the note said that there were hundreds of thousands of citizens protesting in support of the students, who continued to call for democracy and to criticize corruption in the government. Dad's note finished up. *And the amazing thing is, the Beijing TV station is allowed to broadcast this!*

It took half an hour to get to the square – usually a ten minute walk, tops. I don't know how to describe what I saw. Maybe I should have paid more attention in writing lessons last year, although I doubted that my teacher could have described what I was looking at either. I mean, it was *awesome*! The whole square was packed – students, women with baby carriages, men with kids on their shoulders, cops. Lots of cops, most of them just wandering around. A couple of people were still trying to fly kites in spite of the press of bodies. There were huge, long white banners with characters on them and all the sentences, which I couldn't understand, ended with exclamation marks. Dozens of small blue and red tents had been set up as protection from the sun. People shouted over loud-hailers. A lot of the students wore white headbands with writing on them.

It was like a huge carnival where too many people showed up. The popsicle and ice cream vendors made a brave try at pushing their carts through the throng, yelling out, doing a great business. Balloons floated on the ends of tight strings.

The Monument to the People's Heroes was still piled high with wreaths and bunches of wilted flowers. Mao's mausoleum, to the south, seemed to float on a calm sea of bodies.

I started to feel a little claustrophobic and I wondered what would happen if this mammoth flood of people panicked or got mad and they all started to stampede in one direction. Not that the atmosphere was ugly. It was like a crowd on the way in to a ball game or a line up outside a show that everyone was hot to see. It was *electric*.

I knew Dad and Eddie were out there somewhere, trying to capture the festival on tape, doing on-the-spot reports, probably trying to interview students. A lot of them could speak English. There were other journalists in the square. You could pick them out pretty easily. White faces showed up and so did foreign clothes, not to mention cameras on shoulders.

Behind the Monument to the People's Heroes was a large contingent of students. Some were sitting, gathered around portable radios, some standing and talking, others were singing and clapping their hands. As I passed them I heard 'Hello! Hello! Mr. Reporter, come talk to us!'

A guy with a red baseball cap on and a loud-hailer in his hand was talking to me. Well, I thought, why not?

'Hi,' I said.

'What country you are from?' he asked.

'Canada. Canadian Broadcasting Corporation. How about you? What university are you from?'

'People's University.'

'I am from Bei Da,' the guy beside him chimed in. 'Beijing University.'

Already a crowd of students had gathered around us, staring at me and pointing and talking among themselves. I reminded myself that I was supposed to be a reporter.

'What do you hope to accomplish with this demonstration?' I asked, conscious of how stuffy I sounded.

'We have made a union of university students in Beijing,' he said, 'and we have been on strike from classes. All Beijing university students are on strike. We have three demands. We want that the government agrees to talk to us like equals, not treat us like children. Second, they must apologize for violence against students last week.' He pointed toward Zhong Nan Hai, where some students had got roughed up a bit. 'Third, we demand that Xin Hua news reports stop lying about us in newspapers and television.' Xin Hua is the government's official news agency. 'We are not against Communist Party and socialism. We want these things to stay. But we want government to listen to the people and stop the corruption by high officials.'

The students around us nodded and chattered away in Chinese.

'What do those say?' I asked him, nodding towards the signs and banners behind him.

He pointed as he translated. 'Long live democracy. That one, Down with Dictatorship. Over there, Support the Correct Leadership of the Communist Party of China.'

'Do you think the government will listen to you?'

'Students' Union has decided that if the officials do not listen, we will plan bigger demonstration on May Fourth.' Then he yelled something in Chinese and raised his arm, making the 'V' or victory sign with his fingers. I caught the words "May Fourth" but nothing else. A deafening cheer surged from the students round us.

'Why then?' I asked.

'Pardon?'

'Why did you pick that particular day?'

'May Fourth is very important day to all Chinese students and intellectuals. Seventy years ago on May Fourth students from Beijing University began the movement that led to the Communist Revolution.'

I was starting to get frustrated. I was interested in what the guy was saying and I wanted to ask him some more, but the crush of students around us – they were pressing against us as if we were in a crowded bus – was getting on my nerves and making me even more claustrophobic and I didn't have a pen and paper to write down what I was seeing and hearing.

'Listen,' I said. 'Is it okay if I come back and ask you more questions later?'

'Very okay. We are happy to talk to Western reporter.'

'What's your name?'

'Sorry, maybe better I don't give my name.'

'Okay,' I said, shaking his hand. 'Maybe I'll see you again.'

I managed to separate myself from the mass of human flesh and move away from the monument towards the hotel.

It was all too much for me. It was pretty warm out, and, I'll tell

you, pushing through an endless crowd, no matter how festi
they seem, is a tough grind.

I worked my way back to Chang An Avenue and finally to t
hotel. I was glad to get back to the empty suite and enjoy a co
pop.

Tonight we watched it all on the news. Eddie couldn't belie
that the government allowed the TV station to show t
demonstration. I mean, some of the posters and banners we
pretty critical. Dad was taping the news show to send it back
Canada after Eddie did a voice-over commentary about how t
news in China had been so free lately.

It was pretty exciting in the suite that night. Eddie w
laughing, typing up a storm. 'This is the biggest story sin
Liberation!' he crowed. Dad was happy as a little kid
Christmas, taping this, editing that. The enthusiasm w
catching. I began to get interested too, especially after talking
that student. I thought I'd be the last person in the world to g
hooked on politics.

But this wasn't what we learned in school. This was real.

May 5

I was ready yesterday to play reporter. I had my tape recorder with me and something to write on.

It took me quite a while to find the student I talked to last Thursday. I decided to call him Hong, which means "red" in Chinese, because of the red baseball cap he wore. I searched for the red cap as soon as I located the Ren Min Da Xue – People's University – banner. When I found him he was talking to the crowd through a loud-hailer, but I couldn't make out what he was saying.

When he stopped talking and the cheering died down I tapped him on the shoulder.

'Hi,' I said.

He smiled. 'Hello, Canadian friend.'

'I was wondering if you and I could have a talk, and if it would be all right if I tape-record you.'

'Okay.'

Beside him a young woman shook her head and started rattling away in Chinese. He and she talked at each other for a few moments – that's what it seemed like, because they were both talking at once – then he said, 'Okay.'

The press of bodies was on us again. I looked around for a place where we could go and talk more privately and immediately laughed at myself. The sea of people flooded the square completely.

'Well, I was wondering what has happened since I saw you last Thursday.'

'Government has become a little bit reasonable, but not enough. Last Saturday officials had a meeting with student representatives, but it was a phony one. Those so-called students are from the government student unions. They do not represent us. We have formed our own Autonomous Union and officials must speak to us. So far, they refused, so that's why we are here today.'

'What will you do if the officials still won't talk to your people?'

A grim look passed over his face. 'We have something planned.' The woman beside him nodded and the chattering around us went up a notch. A lot of the students understand English.

'How old you are?' said the woman. She wore jeans and a jean jacket, so I figured I'd call her Lan, which means 'blue.'

I didn't want to lie, so I tried changing the subject. 'What do you study in university?' It was a pretty lame question but it worked. She started to talk about university life and Hong threw in a remark now and then.

Lan is twenty and she's from the Foreign Affairs University

where China's diplomats are trained. Hong is twenty-three, a medical student. Lan told me what subjects she studied and all that stuff, but I was more interested in some other facts. While I listened I thought about Lao Xu, I guess because I was hearing the same kind of stuff that Eddie was telling me about Lao Xu's life. Everything is controlled. These students were being told how to run every part of their lives. For example, they weren't supposed to date. They couldn't get married. They had to go to political study classes every week. And if they stepped out of line there were hundreds of thousands of others waiting to take their spots. No wonder they thought that no one listened to them. No wonder they were here.

We talked a bit longer and then I said goodbye. That night on the news we heard that Zhao Zi-yang had made a speech later in the afternoon and said that he thought the situation would calm down and that there would be no turmoil in China.

After the newscast ended we all looked at Lao Xu, waiting for an interpretation. I was beginning to learn that the Chinese often speak in a sort of code so that they don't have to say things straight out.

Lao Xu looked worried. He sighed and said, 'Zhao Zi-yang has broken with Deng Xiao-ping.'

'What!' Eddie shouted.

'Remember the editorial on April 26, Eddie? It came from Deng and it said that the students were promoting chaos. Now Chairman Zhao is saying that there will be no chaos. He has rejected Deng's analysis. That means he has rejected Deng.

'The Communist Party now talks with two voices. That means trouble. Big trouble.'

I wondered where the students and Lan and Hong fit in to all this. Then I realized it. They were right in the middle.

May 20

Things have gotten *really* hairy around here.

I've been so busy I haven't had time to keep this journal every day. Everyone thinks there's a big wind of change blowing, and when the storm passes, I want to remember every second of it.

On May 13 the students in Tian An Men Square changed their tactics. Up until then, thousands had refused to leave the square, and every day the place was a carpet of humanity. But on the thirteenth one thousand students started a hunger strike and vowed to keep it up until either they died or the government promised to meet with their representatives and to begin reforms. When I heard that I rushed down there. The students were set up in the centre of the square, sitting or lying on spread-out newspapers, surrounded by thousands more who were not hunger-striking. The *da zi bao*, the big character posters, demanded that the Communist Party become more democratic and that corruption in the high levels of the Party be stopped.

I spotted Hong and Lan among the strikers, but I couldn't get near enough to talk to them.

Later, when I asked Lao Xu what this stuff about corruption was all about he looked a little bit uncomfortable. He gave me a vague answer about a few bad men being dishonest. Eddie butted in as he usually does.

'Lao Xu is giving you the Party line, Alex. He doesn't want to criticize the government.'

Lao Xu looked even more embarrassed and laughed the way Chinese do when they feel uncomfortable. Eddie shouldn't have centered him out like that, I thought. I let the matter drop until Lao Xu had left. Then Eddie told me that the powerful men and women in the Party got special treatment in everything, from buying foreign goods in special stores that only they could shop in, to housing, to special hospitals or special sections of already existing hospitals that had all the latest medical equipment. They made sure their relatives and children got good jobs and privileges. They sent their kids to universities in Europe, Canada, and the States, all at government expense. And they used government money to fatten themselves. Meanwhile, ordinary people stayed poor.

I remembered that Lao Xu had told me that most of the powerful men in the Party were Long March veterans.

'*All* of them?' I asked. 'Are they *all* crooked?'

Eddie frowned. He didn't like being contradicted. 'They control everything, and they keep most of it for themselves,' he summed up.

Anyway, at least a thousand students started the hunger strike, and a day or so later, two thousand more joined them. Things in our office were pretty frantic. Eddie was going nuts, bossing everybody around, contradicting himself. He was supposed to be covering the upcoming visit of Premier Gorbachev, but he said he knew in his newsman's bones that the student demonstrations were the bigger story. Dad was loving every second of it, spending millions on taxis. He'd dash off to tape the preparations for the state visit, then rush back to see what was going on in the square. Lao Xu seemed busiest of all, one minute translating stuff for Eddie, then running down to meet Dad in the square, then being called back by Eddie on the two-way radio to do something for him. Eventually he slept in the suite with us, which was against hotel regulations, but no one in the hotel seemed to be paying much attention to regulations. It seemed like everybody was having a holiday from regulations.

Me included. I tried to keep up the schoolwork, but I didn't get much done. I skipped school a lot. I went to the square at least twice a day to see what was going on. Sometimes I went with Dad.

Eddie said he figured the students started the hunger strike when they did to embarrass the government. He figured their tactic was to force the government to give in to their demands because the government wouldn't want hunger strikers in Tian An Men Square when Premier Gorbachev arrived. It would look pretty bad, if when the premier came for the required tour of the square and the Forbidden City before going into the Great Hall of the People, three thousand students were laid out on the pavement starving to death.

Dad mimicked a tour leader's nasal voice. 'Here is the Monument to the People's Heroes, and there, just past the students who are starving themselves because they think we're a bunch of old crooks, is the Chairman Mao Memorial.'

When Gorbachev got here for his visit on the fifteenth, all the news reports showed him shaking hands with the Chinese government bigwigs. Everybody smiled so hard I thought their faces would crack. Banquets. Visits to the Great Wall. More banquets. More smiles and handshakes and friendly talks while they sat in deep armchairs with big doilies on the arms and interpreters sitting behind them. There was a whole lot of talk about the renewed friendship between the Russian and Chinese people after a thirty-year break. I didn't see any *xiao ren* – ordinary people – Russian *or* Chinese, on those broadcasts. As far as I could tell, the Chinese people were in Tian An Men Square.

And the Russian premier didn't get to visit the Forbidden City or the square, because the students were still there, lying on the concrete surrounded by their friends and classmates. Too bad, Gorby.

On the second day of Gorbachev's visit the ambulances started coming to Tian An Men Square. I was there. It was a hot sunny morning and the hunger-strikers lay in rows on army-type cots under protective canopies. Some of them had even been refusing fluids and were so weak they couldn't stand or sit.

I tried again to find Lan and Hong, but it was hard to get close and harder still to see the faces of those lying down. But I kept searching. I must have been at it for over an hour before I found them.

I hardly recognized Lan. She looked like a stick-doll. Her eyes had sunk into her head and she sort of stared into nowhere. She was one of those who would not take anything to drink. Hong was on the cot beside her. He still had on his red cap. When I called out to him he got up on his elbow and smiled when he saw me.

'Hello, Canadian friend,' he said weakly. His lips were dry and cracked. 'How are you today?'

'How are *you*?'

'We are in good spirits, although some of us are weak. More and more students are joining the hunger strike every day. We –'

Hong was interrupted by a voice blaring over the loudspeakers the students had set up.

'What was that all about?' I asked him when the noise stopped.

'More ambulances have come,' he said.

About fifteen minutes later, four students took Lan away. As she was being carried through the crowd a woman cried out and tried to clutch Lan's clothing, wailing as though someone had

died. All I could make out was, 'Please, please.' Lan was lifted
into the ambulance. Others were helped in after her. Then the
ambulance crept away, horn braying as it moved slowly through
the crowd.

Hong stayed on his cot, staring up at the canopy above him. I
figured he had one more day until an ambulance took him away
too. I said goodbye to him and he flashed me a victory sign.

Back at the hotel that night I thought a lot about what Hong
and Lan are doing. I can't decide whether they're being really
brave or really dumb. What I am sure of is that it's dangerous. I
guess that's why I admire them so much.

Once the premier had gone, things started to happen fast. Two
of the mega-powerful boys, Li Peng, who is the premier, and
Zhao Zi-yang, the chairman of the Communist Party, visited
some of the hunger-strikers who had been taken to hospital. That
was shown on TV also. Li Peng, with his round, smiling face and
dark-rimmed glasses, was shown going from bed to bed, shaking
hands with the students and talking to them. He looked about as
sincere as a used-car salesman.

On Friday morning before dawn the phone rang. I heard Lao
Xu answer it and start yelling into the receiver. Then he shouted,
'Wake up! There is a rumour that Zhao Zi-yang is going to Tian
An Men Square to talk to the students!'

We were all up and dressed in moments. 'Let's go!' Eddie said.

I grabbed my backpack. No one seemed to notice that I went
right along with them.

The tall light standards in the square and the lights from the
monuments make it easy to see where you're going, although you
need extra lights for TV pictures. It took us at least half an hour to
push through the throng to the Monument to the People's
Heroes, which is where Eddie figured the action would be. Buses
were parked in the square now, commandeered by the students
for shelter when it rained. It was cold out, and a lot of people had
coats on.

Nothing was happening at the monument. Eddie said to Dad,
'Let's split up and call on the two-way if we see anything.'

'Okay,' Dad answered. 'I'll go down towards Qian Men.' That's the Front Gate.

'I'll cover the mausoleum,' Eddie said. 'Lao Xu, let's go.'

'Alex, you can come with me,' Dad said.

'Why don't I stay here? That way we can cover three areas at once.'

'I don't know, Alex. I don't want you to get lost.'

What a lame thing to say, I thought. Eddie must have agreed. 'Are you kidding, Ted? Your kid knows this city better than most of the residents!'

Dad agreed, reluctantly, and the three of them waded into the crowd. I went up to the base of the monument among a hundred or so students and tried to get a look around. The first tier of the tall building still had a lot of wreaths on it. Nothing unusual seemed to be happening – other than probably half a million people, tents, parked buses, voices yelling over loud-hailers, TV lights sparking up for a few minutes then fading again.

I fished my camcorder out of my pack. It would be worthwhile to try taping anything that happened. Then I checked my radio to make sure it was on channel one and that it was on receive mode. I put it in my breast pocket.

I stood around for a while, fighting off the chill, before I noticed something going on over at the Great Hall of the People. A blaze of lights had come on, like a cluster of white torches. Something was up. The lights began to move towards me so I decided to stay put.

I took out my radio and keyed it. 'Dad, Eddie, this is Alex. Can you see the lights? In the northwest quadrant, moving towards me. Over.'

'Alex, Dad here. I can't see them. I'm on the south side of Qian Men. The smell of Kentucky chicken is driving me nuts. Over.'

'And I can't see *anything*,' was Eddie's response.

'I'll check it out and let you know. Over and out.'

I put the radio in my pocket again. The lights were moving towards me quickly. They were TV lights. Somebody important was coming.

Right near the monument was a bus, and when Zhao Zi-yang got to the bus he stopped. He was at the centre of a tight circle of students wearing the white headbands that said *Democracy Now!* in Chinese. He reached up and started shaking hands with students in the bus. Amazing. This guy was the second most powerful man in China.

By that time I was making my way towards him. I had to climb down from the monument's base, so I lost sight of Zhao, but the lights were easy to home in on. What wasn't easy was pushing through the crowd. Then I got an idea. I took off my hat and stuffed it in my pocket so my blonde hair would show.

'Press! Press!' I shouted, and held my camcorder up high so it could be seen. 'Press! Let me through, please!'

It worked. The crowd of students parted and I got to the bus in time to see that Zhao was talking. He was of medium height, with a high forehead and western style glasses. I put the camcorder to my eye and zoomed in to get a medium close-up of Zhao with students at the bus windows in the background. Even through the viewfinder I could see that he was crying as he spoke to the crowd.

The only thing from his speech that I understood were the words . . . 'too late.'

I probably don't need to write down how deliriously happy Dad and Eddie were when I hooked my camcorder up to our office TV and showed them the tape. I thought Eddie was going to carry me around the room.

Within an hour Dad had found someone in the hotel who agreed to take the tape to the satellite feed station and Eddie had written a report and faxed it to Toronto.

I was delirious myself. The reporter's bug had *really* bitten me.

We all wanted to go back to sleep but we couldn't. Too much

to do. I skipped school again. Dad went back to the square with Eddie and Lao Xu to try and interview some students about Zhao's visit and ask them what they thought it meant to their movement. I got to clean up the office because Eddie wouldn't let anyone from the hotel in. Pretty demeaning job for someone who got his video report on national TV, if you ask me.

It took me all morning to tidy up the office. It's hard to make an office neat when you know that the people who work in it are used to a mess and that if they ever came back to find an orderly workplace they'd think they were in the wrong office. I also made sure all the battery rechargers were full and charging away.

After lunch Lao Xu came by and started using the phone as he often did. He tried to catch people after the customary afternoon nap, before the lines got too busy again. He was shouting away for an hour or so, saying '*Wei? Wei?*' about once a second, then he sat and made some notes.

Eddie and Dad came back later in the afternoon, looking tired. Dad put away his camera in its aluminum case and flopped into one of the armchairs. Eddie said hello and headed for the shower with his pipe still in his mouth.

Just as Eddie padded into the office wearing a towel around his large middle and drying his hair with another towel the phone rang. Lao Xu answered it, yelled for a few seconds, listened some more, and hung up, looking glum.

'There is a rumour that Chairman Zhao Zi-yang has been removed from office,' he said quietly. 'And my friend says we should turn on the TV.'

I pushed the button and the screen came to life. We gathered around.

'That's Li Peng,' Lao Xu said. The premier was talking. He looked stern, even angry, but he had a look on his face that seemed to say, 'I'm the boss now.'

'What's up, Lao Xu?' Dad asked.

Lao Xu kept his eyes on the screen. 'Please wait, Ted.'

So the three of us stared at Li Peng, dressed in a dark blue Mao suit, collar buttoned up under his chin, chopping the air with his hand, karate-style, as he talked. I could make out a couple of words, like *China* and *student* and *foreigner*. Then it was over.

Dad and Eddie and I turned to Lao Xu. We knew from the look on his face that the news was not good. He spoke in a low voice, as if he couldn't quite believe his own words.

'Premier Li Peng says that Beijing is now under martial law.'

'Oh-oh,' Dad said.

Eddie let out a low whistle, puffing out his moustache.

Lao Xu continued. 'And he has ordered all students and others to clear Tian An Men Square or face the consequences. Their presence is illegal. All demonstrations are illegal. It is also illegal to spread rumours. And,' Lao Xu added, looking directly into Eddie's eyes, 'foreign correspondents are forbidden to report on anything to do with the students' presence in Tian An Men Square. If they disobey, measures will be taken.'

I knew what martial law meant. It meant that all laws were suspended, even the constitution, and the government made policy directly, using the military to carry it out. Martial law meant soldiers on the street corners with guns, searches of persons and houses without any kind of warrant – by soldiers, not police. It meant curfews. And fear mixed with excitement.

Which is what I was starting to feel.

But a couple of things I didn't understand. 'What's this stuff about rumours?' I asked Lao Xu.

'It means –'

Eddie cut him off. 'Remember what I told you about how the government here controls and manages the news, Alex?' I nodded, a little put out that he was answering for Lao Xu. 'Well, the government will now tell more lies to the people than ever and withhold more information than ever. If people start circulating the truth, they are accused of spreading rumours and arrested. It's a way of controlling information.'

I looked at Lao Xu. He sat there with a glum look on his face and nodded without saying anything.

'What will happen now?' I asked.

In unison, Eddie and Lao Xu shrugged.

'Lao Xu, can you still work for Dad and Eddie?' I wanted to know. 'I mean, won't this make things more difficult for you?'

Lao Xu smiled. 'I can continue,' he answered, 'for the time being, because I have not yet been told anything different by my leader.'

I stood at the office window looking at the crowds streaming along Chang An Avenue. Martial law, I thought. That's what Zhao must have meant when he said, 'It's too late.'

May 21

Last night, after Lao Xu left, Eddie and Dad had a long discussion about the martial law restriction on journalists. For one thing they had to decide whether or not they would continue to send reports about the demonstrations to Canada. That part was pretty short. Eddie said he wasn't about to pass up what could be the biggest story of the decade and maybe the biggest story in China since Liberation in 1949. 'It could even lead to a book,' he added.

I knew what Dad's decision would be. Don't forget, this is the guy who held up thousands of cars on the Gardiner Expressway in rush hour so he could get the capture of some bank robbers on tape.

'Besides,' Dad added, 'I think these kids over here have been peaceful and sensible in this demonstration. No one has been hurt. All they seem to want is for the government to listen to them. We have an obligation to get their story out of the country. If that means breaking martial law, so what? After all, what can the government do to us? Send us home? If we don't cover this we might as well be at home anyway.'

So that was that. They talked longer about Lao Xu. Dad was worried that if they kept covering the story they'd put Lao Xu in a difficult position – the position of a Chinese helping foreigners to break Chinese law. Lao Xu could go to prison for that.

Eddie nodded all the way through Dad's speech, puffing on the stove. 'Yep. I agree. But we should let Lao Xu decide what he wants to do.'

This afternoon Eddie got a phone call telling him that the People's Liberation Army had sent plain clothes men into the radio and TV stations and into the offices of all the newspapers published in Beijing. The PLA, in other words, had taken over the Beijing media. It began to look like Eddie was right about information control.

May 22

The satellite feed to North America and Europe has been shut down by the government. TV pictures can't be sent out of China directly.

Dad was angry. His bright blue eyes snapped. 'This means we'll have to smuggle the tapes out,' he said with determination.

Eddie wasn't surprised. 'After all,' he said, 'the whole thing was set up for Gorbachev's visit. There was an agreement to keep the feed open for a month, with possibility of renewal. So the Chinese government broke the agreement. What else is new?'

May 23

Early this morning Lao Xu went with Dad and me to Tian An Men Square. It was a chilly morning with bright sunshine. Beijing may be under martial law but you'd never know it – except for the military helicopters that buzzed overhead. The students in the tent city were huddled under those long green padded coats that are common here. The square is still packed with people and there are still lots of buses scattered around with students sleeping in them. The students are well organized and seem to have enough food. Lots of the food is brought by local residents.

The temporary latrines have not been replaced, so when the wind is right – or wrong – the square isn't a very pleasant place to be. Signs and banners are everywhere. The atmosphere is calm, as if the demonstrators expect to be there a long time, as if everyone is waiting.

I went to look for Hong first thing, but I guess I had been right about him. He was probably in the hospital.

There seemed to be a lot of meetings going on. We eavesdropped on one. Lao Xu said that the students were discussing tactics. Some said they should obey the martial law ban on demonstrations, some said they should stay, some said they should seal off the square by barricading the streets leading to it. They all seemed to agree that eventually the soldiers will come.

Lao Xu read some of the signs for us. Many of them name the universities represented – Beijing University, Qinghua University, People's University, Beijing Normal University. Some of the signs said Down with Li Peng or Down with Deng Xiao-ping. He's the guy Eddie says really runs the country but there have been lots of rumours that he's sick and might die soon. Some of the signs had little pop bottles hanging from them. Dad asked Lao Xu what they were for.

'Hey! I know!' I cut in. '*Xiao ping* means "little bottle". It's a play on Deng Xiao-ping's name which really means "Little Peace". Right, Lao Xu?'

Lao Xu looked uncomfortable. 'Yes. It's very bad manners. All of these signs calling for down with this person and that are rude. And dangerous.'

Dad wasn't listening. He had the video camera up to his eye. It was pointed at the little bottles.

Things are getting really intense. This morning the PLA tried to enter the city. Their objective, of course, was to clear the square because the demonstrations are a defiance of martial law.

Well, guess what happened? Hundreds of thousands of citizens of Beijing poured out into the streets and blocked the roads! I mean, the roads just filled up with live standing bodies! Nothing could move. People surrounded the trucks and the columns of soldiers and stopped them in their tracks!

I took a little tour on my bike – with the camcorder rigged up and running, naturally – heading west along Chang An, past Xi Dan Street market area where I bought my bike. I didn't even get to the second Ring Road before I met so many people that I had to get off my bike and walk. What I saw was amazing. I saw soldiers sitting on benches in the back of an army truck, looking embarrassed while students standing on the hood of the truck lectured them through loud-hailers. Some students offered the soldiers food or bottles of pop. The soldiers refused them. When I got closer I could see citizens – women with net shopping bags full of vegetables over their arms, old men with those whispy beards – talking with the soldiers at the tailgate.

One interesting thing was that the soldiers weren't armed. I remembered what Lao Xu had told me about the PLA being a people's army. The citizens and students I saw obviously thought so too. They were telling the soldiers to turn around and go away.

And they did! Later in the afternoon the army pulled out of the centre of the city.

As I pedalled along on my way back to the hotel I thought about what I'd seen. What kind of army, I thought, goes into combat – even crowd control – unarmed? What kind of officer allows his men to sit in the back of a truck like kindergarten kids on the way to the zoo while civilians lecture them and laugh at them? Could the Chinese army be *that* incompetent? Was this the army that beat the Guomindang, held off the UN in Korea, skirmished with the Russians along the northern border, and whacked the Vietnamese every so often?

I passed a road sign with some characters and an arrow on it pointing down a side street. The arrow triggered thoughts about Zhu Ge-liang and the way he fooled both Cao Cao and Sun Quan. He did it by feigning one thing and doing another. Classic strategy, I thought. Then I remembered a famous quotation from

Sun Zi's *The Art of War* in the chapter on strategy. Make yourself appear to be weak in order to make the enemy proud and rash, he wrote. Even though you are capable, feign incompetence. The enemy would be put off guard.

Were the PLA playing games with the people? And, in their eyes, were the people now the enemy?

This afternoon while I was out in the streets Lao Xu was called away by his Party boss for a briefing. He returned to tell us that he has been warned not to aid us in anyway if we are breaking martial law.

'Well, that's it, then,' said Eddie. 'You have to stay away, Lao Xu. Because we aren't quitting, and if you stay, you'll be in trouble that you'll never get out of.'

Dad agreed, but Lao Xu said he'd like to stay and help us. He just won't help us directly if we do anything illegal. Eddie argued with him but finally said the decision was Lao Xu's and he would welcome his help if he wanted to stay.

Lao Xu said he wanted to. Dad's twinkling eyes caught mine. I knew what he was thinking. Was Lao Xu staying to help, or to keep an eye on us for the Party?

May 24

I woke up before dawn. I had been tossing and turning, having bad dreams that I forgot as soon as I woke. I felt wrung out and low, like nothing good was going to happen that day and I might as well stay in bed.

But I couldn't. I couldn't get back to sleep no matter how much I tried.

So I got up and wandered into the office. The little red lights on the battery rechargers glared angrily at me like vicious insects. I turned on the light and the red eyes almost disappeared. I shut the door behind me so I wouldn't disturb Dad and Eddie. They were both whacked. They had been working like madmen for the last while.

I made some tea — there's always a big thermos bottle or two full of boiled water in the office — and turned the light off again. The red insect eyes came back to life but I ignored them. I cleared a spot on the top of the desk Lao Xu uses and climbed up, sitting cross-legged with my knees almost touching Eddie's plants, and looked out the window. The street below glowed with pools of amber light from the streetlights. Bikes drifted by. Joggers trundled along in the bike lanes. The odd taxi swooshed past. It was nice and peaceful and quiet.

But I couldn't get rid of the feeling of — I don't know — *dread* is too strong a word, I guess, but that's the idea. I don't even know what caused the feeling. Maybe it was just hangover from whatever nightmare woke me up.

I sipped my tea and watched the street. People. I remembered that impression I had had on the way to see the Great Wall. People. You couldn't look anywhere, across a field in the afternoon, down an alley at night, into a street before dawn, without seeing people. I followed the tail-lights of a taxi speeding west toward the square. There, I knew, thousands of students were camped out, lying on narrow cots or cold concrete, waiting for the dawn. And the soldiers they knew would eventually march on them. It came into my mind again that many of the students are only a year or two older than me. They're trying to change things. People like Lan and Hong are sacrificing a lot to change things. I remembered, too, stories my Dad had told me about his days in university. He had demonstrated, too, about South Africa, environmental stuff. What have I done, so far? Watched TV, listened to the radio, gone to school. Played with toy soldiers.

I stayed perched on the desk, sipping green tea, watching the light leak onto the street from my left, turning it grey, then grey-white. I could tell by the red flags on top of the Great Hall of the People in the distance that the wind was stiffening.

The street below me stepped up its life. Buses snorted along, the bikes came out in force, pedestrians hurried here and there, taxis turned into the hotel parking lot or slipped out into the street and away.

It wasn't too long after that when I realized that something was going on. What tipped me off was that a lot of the pedestrians had stopped moving and soon the sidewalks on both sides of Chang An Avenue were jammed.

It was another demonstration. The marchers came into view from my left, along with the bright sunlight. They filled the street, walking slowly under huge banners which bellied and dipped in the wind. As the procession came by, people from the sidewalks joined in.

I got off the desk to wake Dad and Eddie.

The demonstration turned out to be the biggest yet. More than a million people took part, students, factory workers, women pushing bamboo baby strollers. The banners shouted *Democracy Now!* and *Support the Students!* and *Stop the Corruption!* There were a lot of what Lao Xu called 'rude' posters, too – what I call Down Withs. And there were posters with cartoons on them, showing Deng Xiao-ping and his two sons driving Mercedes Benz cars, and other guys I didn't recognize counting stacks of money.

In the afternoon I was up on the roof with Dad, who was, naturally, watching everything through the lens of his Betacam, when the big wind – the *da feng* – started to blow. Then the rain came. The storm turned vicious fast, driving the rain like nails, drenching us in minutes. We went back to the suite and watched from the windows, wiping the steam away with wet hands. The marchers didn't quit. They kept it up, flowing slowly, like cold syrup, towards the square, hanging on to their posters and banners like drowning sailors.

May 25

Today Beijing Radio broadcast a report on yesterday's big demonstration. Lao Xu translated for us and I taped his translation. The report was telling about the demonstration as if only a few thousand people had been involved. It didn't say that workers from the factories took part, or ordinary citizens. It gave the impression that the demonstrators were all rebellious students and 'bad elements' and 'hooligans.'

I was laughing at those 1930s gangster-movie terms when I noticed Lao Xu's face go pale. His mouth dropped open and he stopped translating.

He just stared at the screen for a moment, then he whispered, 'No, no.'

Dad noticed before Eddie did. 'What's the matter, Lao Xu?'

Lao Xu gulped and said so low I could barely hear him over the voice on the TV. 'The government has said that the student demonstrators are counter-revolutionaries!'

'My god,' Eddie gasped. 'My god. Now they're really in for it.'

Dad looked as confused as I felt. But he and I had been in China long enough to know that propaganda labels mean a lot. 'What does that mean exactly?'

'It means,' Lao Xu answered, 'that the student demonstrators are enemies of the state. It means that if they are arrested they can be shot.'

'What?' I shouted. 'Enemies? Shot? That's dumb! They haven't done anything wrong! They're just trying to improve things!'

Dad chimed in, 'But all the demonstrations have been remarkably peaceful, Lao Xu.'

Lao Xu suddenly looked tired. 'I know, Ted. But none of that matters now. If the students don't leave the square . . .'

Eddie was already banging away on the computer. He talked while he typed, his hands a blur. 'They'd better leave,' he said. 'They'd better. Ted, get the fax ready, will you?'

May 26

Rumours, rumours, rumours.

It's hard to sort out all the rumours. One says that Deng Xiao-ping is seriously ill and the Chinese embassies around the world have been notified to expect an announcement of his death. Another says he's already dead and the power struggle to replace him has started and the hard-line conservatives, headed by Li Peng, are in control. Another says he's healthy and is hiding in Sichuan, his native province, to keep distant from the turmoil so he doesn't get his hands dirty if something bad happens.

Two rumours are solid. One, the army has Beijing surrounded.

Soldiers have been moving into the area again since martial law was declared six days ago. I got out my map of the city and showed Dad and Eddie where soldiers would probably be massed. One place would be the main railway station on East Qian Men Street, not too far from Tian An Men Square. Another would be the Wu Lu railway station to the west of the city. I figured this because, in China, there isn't a big network of highways like there is in North American cities, so the main way to move people and produce and stuff is the trains. They'd probably use military airports, too, but they were too far away to be on my map.

I hopped on my bike and checked out the main railway station myself. I came at it from the south and scanned the huge network of rails with binoculars. Sure enough, there were dozens and dozens of railway cars resting on the sidings with thousands of soldiers sitting outside cooking noodles on open fires, washing clothes in little wash basins, doing what all soldiers have to know how to do – wait. It was awesome. I almost wished I could be one of them. Then I remembered Lan and Hong and why the army was in Beijing.

The Wu Lu station was too far away to reconnoiter, but I was pretty sure there would be the same scene there.

Eddie and Lao Xu went down to the square to see how the students were responding to the news. The demonstrators were shocked that the government had said they were counter-revolutionaries. There were lots of meetings going on to decide what to do.

'A couple of thousand students have vowed not to leave the square until the government reforms itself,' Eddie told us, 'but a lot of the students – maybe most – have already left. Who can blame them?'

May 27

Things were pretty quiet today. We heard more rumours that tanks and armoured personnel carriers have massed on the outskirts of the city but, as Eddie says in his newspaper-ese, we haven't been able to confirm these reports.

As soon as he said that, though, he added, 'There's something going on here that's a lot bigger than student demonstrations.'

How come the heavy-duty hardware? When I saw the PLA on the twenty-third they weren't even armed. Tanks? Armoured personnel carriers? Seems pretty demented to me.

May 28

Something's up.

Students are beginning to come back to the square. Not in demonstrations or parades, but in trickles, and from all directions. Dad and I were down there this afternoon. Dad wanted to get some shots of the square after the students – most of them, that is – had left. We expected to find a desolate and messy expanse of concrete. But we didn't. It soon became clear that a lot of students had come back. They're still coming. What's going on?

The rumours about the heavy-duty hardware have been confirmed.

May 29

The square is packed with humans again. It's pretty tense down there. Everyone is wondering what will happen next.

This afternoon a bunch of those three-wheeled bicycle transports with the platforms in back arrived, inching through the crowds, with huge white objects on them.

This evening, after dark, we all went down to the square again. The white things had been fitted together to make a statue. It's a tall white figure of a woman, much like the Statue of Liberty in the States, only she's using two hands instead of one to hold up the torch. Lao Xu says the students are calling her the Goddess of Democracy.

What's really interesting is where they put her. She's standing in front of the Gate of Heavenly Peace, where Mao Ze-dong declared the founding of the People's Republic of China in October 1949 and where his big picture hangs now.

And she's staring at the picture of Mao right in the face.

May 30–June 2

Things are really intense.

Journalists are going nuts, talking together in the hotel coffee shop, faxing photos of the goddess and reports of the latest developments to their papers and TV stations, trying to find tourists who will smuggle videotapes to Hong Kong, Japan, Europe – anywhere. As soon as they're out of China the tapes can be couriered back home or, better still, sent by satellite.

Chinese radio and TV are still railing against the students, calling them counter-revolutionaries, accusing them of trying to destroy the economic reforms of the last ten years, telling the citizens the demonstrators are all hooligans. But the people aren't buying it.

More rumours. The Beijing police have refused to clear the students out of the square or to tear down the goddess. The government is going to send in the troops again.

And they did. Tonight, after dark, the troops tried to come in. The word went up and down the streets like an electric current. People poured out of apartment blocks and *hu tongs* and flooded into the streets, bringing all traffic to a halt. Dad and I and Eddie left the hotel and rushed east along Chang An Avenue. We didn't get far before we saw the crowds. It was like the people were a sea and each truck in the column was the tip of an island.

And the people were an angry sea – not like last time. They shouted and waved their fists at the soldiers in the trucks. I wondered why. I couldn't understand what they were shouting.

Dad was standing behind a tree, holding the camera against the trunk so it wouldn't be too conspicuous, getting it all on video. We knew the pictures wouldn't be very good quality, but we also knew this was too good to miss.

I got as close as I could to the trucks. A bolt of excitement hit me. No wonder the people were angry. This time, the soldiers were armed! Each one carried an AK 47 machine gun. And each AK 47 had a wicked-looking bayonet fixed to the barrel. The PLA wore helmets and those big ammunition pouches on their chests.

They didn't look bewildered and embarrassed the way the soldiers had on the twenty-third. They looked tough. And mad. This time they looked like *real* soldiers, not those kids in green who 'guarded' the doors of the Great Hall of the People or those wimps who sat in the trucks and got an earful from the civilians.

The stalemate lasted for about three hours. Then the trucks reversed, turned around, and withdrew.

The citizens, and the students, had won again. What an army, I thought. They lost face again. They looked stupid. I was glad.

June 3

This morning I was grounded.

I came back early from school because classes have been postponed indefinitely. Most of the diplomats pulled their kids out because they don't think it's safe enough to send them to school. It's just as well, I guess, because I've been missing classes quite a bit lately. My tones are probably really lousy now.

I got back home to find Eddie and Dad deep into a conversation that stopped short when I came through the door. They both looked at me guiltily, so I knew something was up.

And here's what they cooked up. Eddie wanted to go down into

he square again. Rumours said the army was going to make
another try.

'Great,' I put in, 'I'll go with you. I don't want to miss
that.'

Nope. The plan was that I would stay in the hotel!

'We need you here,' Eddie explained. And he went on to say
that he and Dad would go down with their two-way radios.
I would stay in the office as a sort of base co-ordinator and,
when I got something interesting from one of them, make an oral
memo into my little tape recorder. Eddie said this would be a
great way to record details for his book while at the same time
letting him get on with his immediate job – E.N.G., Electronic
News Gathering.

Dad nodded all the way through this line of nonsense but I
could see from the look in his eye that he knew I wasn't buying
it.

'This is just an excuse to keep me here, right? Because you
think it will be too dangerous, right?'

Dad didn't say anything.

Eddie said, 'No, really, Alex, you'd be more useful to us up
here.'

'Come on, Eddie, you could take the tape recorder with you
and make the memos yourself down there. You don't need me to
do that.'

'Yeah, I could, Alex, but you're forgetting something.'

'I'll bet. What?'

'Point of view. If I do it, all we'll have is what *I* see. From up
here you can record your dad's observations, mine, and anything
Lao Xu gets over the telephone.'

I thought hard but I couldn't argue my way out of that
one.

Eddie hammered his point home. 'Your dad and I will take our
Polaroids with us and try to get pics we can fax home. And we'll
send you oral reports of what's going on. Not having to stop and
write leaves us free to move fast. I've got a feeling we're going to
see a lot of action today.'

I couldn't think of anyway out of it. I wanted to go with them

and be in the middle of things, right where it was happening – i
anything *did* happen – not stuck in a hotel room yapping into
tape recorder.

Dad was talking. 'Alex, I *would* rather have you up here in case
anything happens, but we also need you to do this. Okay?'

'Okay, Dad.' What else could I say?

They left about ten o'clock, dressed in Chinese hats and blue
Mao coats. Eddie wasn't fooling anybody, though. For one thing
you have to walk a lot of miles before you'll find a chubby
Chinese man, and even Eddie's coat couldn't hide his thick body
and potbelly. For another, his florid complexion would be like
a flashing red light. Dad didn't look convincing, either. He was
much too tall and gangly.

I set up shop on Eddie's desk. I had a pad to take notes so I
wouldn't miss details when I got the reports. I had the two-way
radio on receive mode and my little tape recorder with fresh
batteries and a new tape. I had batteries cooking on the recharger
right on the desk, and a couple of spare tapes.

And nothing happened.

What a letdown. Well, Eddie called in to report that he was
going to hang around the Great Hall of the People, and on the
way there he radioed that the goddess was still standing there
staring Mao in the face, and thousands of people were milling
around her, including dozens of foreign correspondents. Dad
called in to say he was going to hang around the south end of the
square. I called back to tell him he probably picked that spot
because that is where the chicken restaurant is.

Lao Xu came in about noon and did a little paperwork. Then
he got a chess set out of his bag. He unfolded the paper board on
the desk beside my stuff and laid out the round pieces with the
characters carved into the tops. He has been patiently teaching
me Chinese chess lately. We started to play.

I wasn't too interested, though. While I waited for him to move
I was fiddling with the channel selector on the two-way when
suddenly I heard this:

  . . . just in front of the Yan Jing Hotel and I can see troops in the distance
  moving towards the centre of Beijing. They must have broken through the
  barricade at the moat at Mu Xi Di. A crowd has already begun to gather.

Yes, people are pouring into the streets, moving east, towards the troops. I'm going to try to get to the roof of the hotel. Over.

Lao Xu's eyes snapped up from the chess game. 'Who is that, Shan Da? Not Ted or Eddie.'

'No, it isn't. I got that over channel five. Hang on a sec.'

I switched back to one. 'Dad, this is Alex. Over.'

'Got you, Alex. Feeling bored? The chicken is great, hah, hah. Has Lao Xu arrived yet?'

'Eddie, can you hear me too? Over.'

'Loud and clear. You sound like you won the lottery. What's up? Over.'

'I just picked up a voice on channel five from someone at the Yan Jing Hotel. He says troops are moving towards the centre of the city. Just a minute. Over.'

'Supposed to say "Stand by," not "Just a minute," ' Dad joked. Lao Xu had pulled the map of Beijing closer and put his finger on the location of the Yan Jing Hotel.

'Dad, this is Alex. That hotel is on Fu Xing Men Avenue. That's the western extension of Chang An. The hotel is west of the Second Ring Road. The troops must be moving in from Wu Lu train station. Over.'

'Alex, Eddie. Okay, monitor that channel and get down everything you can. Pass it on to us and we'll let people here know. Must be a reporter you've picked up. Over.'

'Okay, Eddie. Over.'

Wow! This was great! I looked at my watch. Two o'clock. I made some quick notes and switched to channel five.

. . . clear view of the scene now. The street is jammed with citizens who are trying to halt the progress of the troops as they have before. The first few ranks of troops have long truncheons –

'What's that word?' Lao Xu cut in.

'Truncheon? It's like a club. Cops use them for crowd control.'

Lao Xu frowned. 'But the PLA would never –'

. . . tear gas cannisters . . . Yes, I can see the white smoke. The troops are using tear gas. The crowd has begun to fall back somewhat, but the wind is blowing the gas off the street, away from the people. The crowd is surging towards the troops again. Some are throwing what looks like rocks. The entire expanse of the street is a mass of people. I can hear them now.

I could hear the roar of the crowd over the radio, too. I switched quickly to channel one and passed the information on to Dad and Eddie. Then I switched back to five.

. . . have begun to attack the crowd with truncheons swinging. People are falling and being dragged away from the melee and onto the sidewalks. The crowd is giving ground, but not much. It appears at this point to be pretty much of a standoff. Over.

I left the radio on channel five and made some quick notes. Then, with an ear to the radio, I talked into the tape recorder.

When I stopped, Lao Xu said, 'Why not record that channel directly, Shan Da? I'll do that for you.'

He moved the chess set out of the way while I talked to Eddie and Dad. Then I signed off and sat back in my chair. I looked over at Lao Xu.

'What do you think is happening?'

Lao Xu looked worried. He ran his fingers through his brush cut.

'Same thing as before, Shan Da. PLA is under orders to clear Tian An Men square. The demonstration there is illegal. And the government is losing face, especially after that statue was put up. I'm afraid there will be big trouble, Shan Da.'

'But you said the PLA would never attack the citizens, right?' As soon as I said that I felt stupid. According to the anonymous voice on channel five the PLA *was* moving in with truncheons and tear gas.

Lao Xu's voice got louder and higher pitched. 'I've seen what happens in situations like this. The crowd will lose control. Nothing good can happen from this!'

He slumped back in his chair and let out a long sigh. '*Shuang fang xiang chi bu xia,*' he murmured.

'Pardon?'

'Neither side will give in.'

'Alex? Eddie here. Over.'

I grabbed the radio and keyed it. 'I hear you, Eddie. Over.'

Eddie was breathing hard. As he talked, his voice shook as if he was running or walking fast.

'I'm heading towards the south-west corner of the Great Hall.

Apparently troops have been seen there.' Lao Xu and I sat up straight in our chairs. 'Ted, you on? Over.'

'I hear you, Eddie. Over.'

'You stay put for now. There might be some movement from the main train station. Over.'

'Okay, Eddie. Over.'

I quickly switched to five.

. . . continues to be a standoff, here. Troops have gained maybe thirty metres in the last fifteen minutes. They've tried tear gas again but . . .'

Back to one.

'. . . on the street that runs north/south behind the Great Hall. Troops are here, all right. Hard to say where they came from. They're completely stalled by thousands of people. Lots of shouting, fist-waving. Students are trying to control the crowd, using electric megaphones.'

'Eddie, Alex. Are the troops armed? Over.'

'I can't see any with guns. I can't see much, Alex. Wait! Yes, the troops on the front rank are slashing at people with their belts.' In a flash I remembered Lao Xu's story about the Red Army on the Long March, boiling and eating their belts as they tried to avoid starvation when they were crossing the Grasslands. 'I don't see any trucks, but there must be some off on the side streets. Okay, now I see truncheons being used. This is amazing. The street is absolutely jammed with people. It's as if someone drew a line about fifty metres from where I'm standing. On one side are the troops trying to move forward. On the other are thousands of men and women. So far it's passive resistance. No one is throwing anything or –'

'I've got something here, Alex! Over!' It was Dad.

I was furiously jotting down what Eddie was saying, holding the radio in my left hand, a ballpoint in my right. Lao Xu had taken over the recorder and was talking into it quietly. I had a strange thought. I wondered if he was censoring what he was putting on tape. Right away I felt ashamed of myself.

'Go ahead, Dad. Over.'

'I'm right in front of the Qian Men. I can see down the street to my left towards the train station. The troops are coming and

students are streaming towards them. I'm off! Wish me luck
Over.'

It went on like that for five hours. The guy at the Yan Jing
Hotel came on every fifteen minutes or so. Things there didn't
change too much. The soldiers kept lobbing tear gas, but the
wind reduced its effectiveness so the citizens surged back, only to
be beaten with truncheons. At Eddie's skirmish, the same thing
but without the tear gas. He figured the army didn't want tear
gas floating around right outside the Great Hall. Dad was right
in the thick of things on Qian Men Avenue West. He estimated
that about twelve hundred troops were trying to get to the square
from that direction. The students held them back. But they were
paying a price.

Eddie and the guy at the Yan Jing Hotel talked mostly in calm
media voices almost as if they were reporting a Kiwanis Club
picnic. But Dad sounded like a kid *at* the picnic.

Then, as if all three battles were on the same frequency, the
troops started to withdraw. On the two-way we could hear the
crowds cheering. In the office, where Lao Xu and I had been
furiously writing and listening and talking for hours, it was as if
a strong wind had suddenly died. The radio reports grew more
and more calm and reports were farther apart. Finally Eddie
came on.

'Ted? Alex?'

Dad and I answered him.

'Let's regroup back at the hotel. Over.'

'Ted here. Okay, see you back there. I'll bring the chicken, but
it's a little spoiled. Tear gas. Over.'

I looked at Lao Xu. I think both of us were wondering if things
really *were* over.

Dad looked pretty wiped when he came into the suite. His
wrinkled dark blue Mao jacket hung on his long frame like a rag
on a stick. Eddie didn't look much better. They flopped down in
their armchairs and sighed.

I went to the fridge and cracked open a couple of beers for them.

'Alex, you're an angel of mercy,' Eddie said when I handed him the glass. Dad just smiled and took a long swallow.

While Dad and Eddie took turns in the shower and got into some fresh clothes, Lao Xu and I rustled up some food for them — stuff we had bought in the shops in the lobby, like crackers, some imported cheese that made Lao Xu wrinkle his nose when we opened it, a can of fish called dace that's smoked and canned with black-bean sauce. It wasn't exactly the kind of picnic that ants would fight over, but Dad and Eddie tore through the food in a few minutes, washing it down with beer, talking fast, interrupting each other, winding down from the excitement of the clash between the soldiers and the citizens.

'Well, what do you think, Lao Xu?' Eddie said after everyone had been silent for a moment, 'I guess we've seen all we're going to see tonight. Think the army will try again before tomorrow?'

Lao Xu was still looking pretty shocked and saddened by it all. 'I don't know, Eddie. I just don't know.'

'I wonder what's going to happen,' Dad said for the hundredth time. 'I can't see the army getting back on the trains and going back to wherever they came from, can you?'

Eddie and Lao Xu shook their heads. 'According to the rumours, there are troops here from all over the country. A guy from AP told me tonight that one army from Harbin had been told they were coming to Beijing to make a movie!'

Lao Xu cleared his throat. 'One thing that is important, Eddie, is that the troops you saw tonight were not Beijing troops.'

Eddie raised his eyebrows.

'What's the diff?' I asked. 'And how do you know?'

Eddie smiled without humour. 'Never ask Lao Xu where he gets his info, Alex.'

Lao Xu explained. 'The PLA don't wear any insignia that tells what army or division they belong to. But I heard that the Beijing troops have been pulled back because they failed to clear the square.'

'Clear the square?' Dad exclaimed. 'They didn't even get near it!'

That's when I remembered the other night – it seemed like a week ago – when we saw the soldiers trapped by a sea of people on Jian Guo Men Avenue. They were armed. The first troops we saw were not.

Lao Xu went on. 'So it is an escalation in the conflict when troops from outside the city are brought in. Maybe that's why the students and the people have been working so hard building more barricades.'

'I get the impression,' Dad said, 'that *all* the streets that lead to the square are barricaded.'

'Apparently.'

'Lao Xu,' Eddie asked, 'does the number twenty-seven mean anything to you?'

'Twenty-seven? What do you mean?'

'Well, you know how lousy my Chinese is, but tonight, when I was on my way back across the square to the hotel, a student was running along yelling something through a loud-hailer. All I could make out was "twenty-seven." '

Lao Xu slowly put down his glass. He swallowed. 'I hope not,' he said in a low voice.

Eddie's eyes lit up the way they always do when he sniffs a story. 'Why?'

'The Twenty-seventh Field Army is based in Hebei Province and is led by Qian Guo-liang, the son-in-law of President Yang Shang-qun. They are hardened troops. Many of them have seen action in Vietnam. They have the reputation of being very tough and bitter because they are mostly illiterate and fanatically loyal to their leader.'

'Ah-hah!' Eddie exclaimed. 'I knew there was more going on here than a student demonstration.'

I didn't get it for a moment. Then it started to fit together. I knew from my reading that the PLA was still, in spite of so-called modernization, a primitively organized army with ten major units made up of twenty armies from around the country. Most of the armies are loyal to individual leaders rather than to the central government. Back before Liberation, far back into Chinese history as a matter of fact, leaders with their own armies were called 'war-lords'. That's really what Cao Cao had been.

Lao Xu was talking again. 'The army that tried to get to the square a few days ago was the Thirty-eighth, the Beijing Garrison. They are mostly city kids. Apparently they refused to go farther when the citizens surrounded them those times.'

'So you think,' Dad said to Eddie, 'that the armies are surrounding the city for more reason than getting the students out of the square?'

Eddie nodded. 'I think that all the players are getting their chess pieces set up on the board, waiting for the game to start.'

Lao Xu said, almost to himself, 'When the Gang of Four were deposed and arrested after Chairman Mao's death in 1976, first the city was surrounded with troops. Then the arrests happened. And the man who led the armies then was —'

'Was our little friend Deng Xiao-ping,' Eddie cut in. 'The guy who now runs the whole country. The guy who is said to be on his deathbed.'

'So if Deng *is* dying, some people are getting ready to move into power,' Dad mused.

'Yep, and if he *isn't*, he's behind all this troop movement and making sure that moderates like Zhao Zi-yang are ousted.'

'And either way,' I put in, 'the students are just being used.' My eye caught the remains of my and Lao Xu's chess game. 'The students are pawns.'

Eddie and Dad looked at each other for a split second before they both got up.

'We have a long night ahead of us,' Eddie said as he walked to the desk. 'Alex, help me get my gear together, will you?'

'This time,' Dad announced, 'I'm taking my camera.'

Lao Xu was wringing his hands. His face was drawn and pale.

'What's wrong, Lao Xu?'

He looked up at me. 'I am afraid, Shan Da. I'm afraid maybe the *da feng* has come again.'

June 4

We used the same system as we did earlier in the evening, and I liked it about as much. I was hot to go back to Tian An Men Square with Dad and Eddie but they used the same arguments against me as they had before. Lao Xu was really worried they'd get into trouble if they were caught reporting on the events in the square and he tried to insist that he should go with them in case they needed an interpreter to get them out of a jam. Eddie said no to him too.

So Lao Xu and I sat frustrated at the desk, with the tape recorder, the two-way, a pad and pens, and the chess set. The office was like a dimly lit cave. We only had one desk lamp turned on because we wanted to be able to see down into the street and it's too hard to see down there if the office is lit up like a dance hall.

Eddie situated himself on the southeast corner of the square, where Dad had been earlier in the evening. Dad wanted to photograph the Goddess of Democracy. He said over the two-way that he got some terrific mood shots, with the Goddess all lit up and surrounded by thousands of students and citizens. He commented that the students still seemed really well organized. The mood down there was tense. Everyone, he said, was waiting for the army to come. A lot of people were strengthening the barricades. Buses and cars couldn't get past anymore, of course. After Dad hung around the goddess for a while he went west to the corner of Chang An Avenue, right in front of the Great Hall of the People.

Leave it to my dad, I thought, to break the law right out in the open, in the most conspicuous spot possible.

By midnight my body wanted to lie down and call it a day but my brain wouldn't let it. I was worried about Dad. I kept thinking what a nut he is, and if he got arrested, he'd probably ask them to let him tape the trial.

About 12:30 A.M. I found out that the guy who had been broadcasting from the Yan Jing Hotel that afternoon was an American from ABC. We talked for a minute or two after I heard him signing on with his colleagues. He was now at the Min Zu Hotel, which is a couple of blocks east of the Yan Jing. He said that ABC had four reporters covering the story – him, a woman in the square somewhere, a man near Zhong Nan Hai, which is just a bit west of the Forbidden City and is where the Party bigwigs live – and guess where their base was? The Beijing Hotel! Two floors below us! We agreed to keep in touch. He sounded almost as nervous as I felt.

I tried to get interested in the chess game Lao Xu and I had started. Lao Xu kept tapping his long thin fingers on the desk and flinching every time the radio crackled. I couldn't concentrate. Finally we gave up the game. He sat on the couch and leafed

through a *China Reconstructs* magazine – not too interested
obviously, because he didn't even turn on the lamp.

After a few minutes he closed the magazine and tossed it onto
the coffee table. He lay down in the shadows, his head resting on
the arm of the couch. His narrow chest rose and fell gently. His
brow was creased. His mouth was a straight tense line.

I thought about Lao Xu and what he'd been through the last
couple of days. His beloved PLA didn't seem to be acting the way
he had told me it would. All his life he had believed in them. His
dad had been an army man who had survived the Long March.
A hero. They were all heroes to Lao Xu.

And I knew he was walking a really tight line with us. Eddie
might be right about him being a spy, but Lao Xu had stuck with
us for more reasons than surveillance. I was convinced of that
now. It was as if he wanted to help explain what was happening so
that we wouldn't get the wrong idea. Who was he trying to
convince, I thought. Us, or himself?

As I watched him trying to rest, it suddenly struck me how
much I liked him. He was intelligent and a scholar, but he wasn't
snobby about it. He had a great sense of humour. And he was
really kind to all three of us, especially me. He was my
friend.

I started doodling nervously on the pad, sitting in a little pool
of yellow light in a hotel room in the middle of a strange city,
thousands of miles away from home, waiting for something to
happen. And mad, because if anything did happen, I wouldn't
be there.

'Shan Da,' Lao Xu said from the couch, 'maybe we should
turn on TV and . . .'

. . . *armoured personnel carrier is approaching the barricade just outside
the hotel. Red and white flares have been fired into the sky, giving off a
harsh eerie light.*

I dropped my pen and turned on my tape recorder. 'Lao Xu!'
I hissed.

The couch creaked as he jumped up and hurried to the
desk.

Thousands of people are in the street, some lining the sidewalks, some behind the barricade across Chang An Avenue. It looks like they are throwing rocks and bricks at the personnel carrier. The carrier has struck the barrier and climbed it. The crowd is parting like water as the carrier picks up speed. It's heading towards the square now. Over.

I snatched up the two-way and switched to channel one. 'Dad! Eddie! Can you hear me? Over.'

They answered. I told them what I'd heard. I wrote 1:00 A.M. on the pad.

'I see it – and hear it – coming this way,' Dad said excitedly. 'The crowd here is massed across the avenue in front of the barricade of buses. They're actually running *towards* the personnel carrier!'

I heard some scratchy noise and then Dad's muffled voice came back on. 'I've put the two-way in my pocket so I can use the camera. Hope you can hear me, Alex. The carrier . . . yes, the carrier has been stopped by the thousands of people in the street. They've surrounded it! Someone has tossed a molotov cocktail under it and the flames have already started to engulf it. The crowd is forced back by the heat. I can't . . . a couple of students have climbed onto the carrier. Beautiful! I can see their white headbands. They're helping the men inside the carrier to get out. This is great! I'm getting all of it!'

Dad was so excited he didn't seem to realize that with his two-way transmit button locked on I couldn't talk to him.

'The soldiers appear to have gotten out safely and away from the burning personnel carrier. The students have disarmed the soldiers and they seem to have disappeared into the crowd. I'm going to stop shooting now.'

I heard the scratching and scraping again and Dad's voice came in, clearly now. 'Did you get all that, Alex? Over.'

'Got it, Dad. Over.'

'Eddie? Over.'

'Yeah, I picked you guys up. Nothing here so far. Over.'

Lao Xu was seated beside me now, talking softly into the tape recorder and making notes to himself in quick, scrawly Chinese characters. I wrote down 1:10 and switched to five.

. . . at least fifty trucks filled with troops, moving slowly from the west.

They are temporarily stymied by the hastily rebuilt barricades and by the crowds . . .

Back to one. Dad's voice: '. . . setting fire to the buses that are ranged across Chang An just in front of me . . . I can't tell who's doing it. Over.'

'Dad, I just got a report that *fifty* trucks full of troops are headed your way. You'd better move out. Over.' I closed my eyes and added to myself, Dad, please, for once, be sensible.

1:20, channel five. . . . *making their way slowly around the barriers. They are not stopping for the citizens in their way. I've seen at least two people crushed under the wheels of the trucks. I repeat. The troop trucks are driving into the crowds! They are not stopping. The crowd is parting reluctantly, letting them by . . .*

'Dad, get out! The troops are on their way! Over!'

'Yes, I see them, Alex. I can see the trucks coming. The crowd is surging west to meet them. I'll be okay. Over.'

'Alex! Ted! I can hear shooting! I can hear shooting! It's coming from somewhere south of the square! Over.'

Lao Xu's strained voice cut in. 'No, no. He must be mistaken. The PLA wouldn't shoot at the people!'

I was already on my feet. I ran into the bedroom and grabbed my backpack. The camcorder was still in it. I rushed back into the living room and yanked battery packs out of the chargers and tossed them in the bag with some 8mm videotapes. I threw on my Mao jacket and pulled my cap on. I dashed to the desk, grabbed the tape recorder, and stuffed it into my jacket pocket. When I picked up the two-way Lao Xu finally clued in to what I was doing.

'Shan Da, no! You must stay here!'

'He won't leave the square, Lao Xu. I know he won't. The only way I can get him out of there is to drag him out.'

'He'll come back soon, Shan Da. He will!'

'You don't know him, Lao Xu. He'll forget about everything except getting pictures. I've got to go get him out! I'm not staying here while he's down there!'

Lao Xu searched my face for a moment. I guess he realized

he'd have to tie me up and gag me to get me to stay. He went to the door and threw on his own sports jacket.

'Then I must go with you.'

'Okay, let's go.'

'Wait. Tell Eddie and your father what we're doing.'

'No way. By the time we finish arguing, I'll be twenty-three years old.'

We tore out of the suite and down the hall. We got down to the lobby to find a couple of hundred people massed in front of the hotel doors gawking into the street, all talking at once. We shoved rudely through the crowd and ran out onto Chang An Avenue. Once there we found that running was impossible. So we threaded and shouldered our way through the masses of bodies as fast as we could. To the west of us we could see flames with wicked black smoke roiling up from them. That must be the buses and armoured personnel carrier burning, I thought.

We had almost reached the statue of the Goddess of Democracy when Dad came on the radio. 'The troops are dismounting from the long line of trucks and forming up. They have AK 47s with fixed bayonets. They look like they mean business. Over.'

I realized that I was holding the radio in one hand and the tape recorder in the other. I looked at my watch. 1:40 A.M. I talked into the recorder.

'. . . coming towards me! I think they've seen the camera.'

Lao Xu and I stopped. We were opposite the Gate of Heavenly Peace. The goddess stood to our right in a blaze of white light. Between me and my dad were thousands of people and a barricade of burning buses lighting up the western reaches of the square.

'. . . after me!'

I held the two-way to my ear. I could hear my dad running and a lot of yelling in Chinese. Then I heard a crash.

'No! Don't!' A smashing sound. More yelling in Chinese. 'Alex! They've –' Dad let out a blood-chilling scream. The radio squealed, then went dead.

I barged through the crowd towards the burning buses. Lao Xu was right beside me.

'They got Dad!' I cried.

Nearer the Great Hall of the People the crowd was thicker, if that was possible. We pushed through, got onto the sidewalk and stopped in front of the huge building. We could see the troops lined up right across Chang An Avenue. I looked around frantically, thinking I might see Dad somewhere. Lao Xu was talking rapidly to people around us and they were shaking their heads.

I keyed the radio. 'Eddie? Alex here. Over.'

'Got you, Alex. Hey! You'll never guess what I saw a minute ago. A guy walking around with a kid up on his shoulders, sightseeing. You'd have thought he was at Ontario Place! He –'

'Eddie,' I heard my own voice shaking, 'I think Dad's been arrested. He might be badly hurt. Over.'

Eddie was all business. For once I was glad of his take-charge tone. 'Alex, you stay put, you hear? If he's been picked up, Lao Xu and I can make a call. I'm going to head back now. I'll be there as soon as I can. Over.'

Eddie thought we were still in the hotel. As soon as he signed off we heard gunfire coming from the south.

I've heard a lot of gunfire on TV and in the movies and it's mostly pretty exciting, with a lot of *pow* and *rat-tat-tat* and the *zing* of ricochets. It doesn't sound anything like what we heard echoing through the dark troubled city that night. The machine-gun bursts sounded as if someone far away was beating rapidly on hollow log with hard batons.

There were two long bursts that seemed to go on forever. Probably they lasted five seconds each. The crowd around us started screaming in rage. You didn't need Chinese to know what angered them. Guns, used by Chinese against Chinese. Out in the street the phalanx of PLA began to move towards the square, slowly, stepping in unison. The long wide column was lit by the eerie orange-red light from the flaming buses. They held their AK 47s at waist level, bayonets forward. The flickering orange-red light made them look cold and mechanical.

The crowd let them get about twenty yards, then started throwing things – stones, bottles, anything. Individuals would burst from the crowd in the street and hurl something, then disappear back into the mass of people.

'Shan Da, we must leave!'

I stuffed the radio, still on receive mode, and the tape recorder into my pockets and struggled out of my pack. I pulled out the camcorder and shouldered the pack again. I looped the camcorder's strap tightly around my wrist and started to record the machine-like advance of the soldiers, not thinking, possessed by the idea that I had to get this on tape, thinking, people have to see this, people have to know this happened.

Lao Xu was yanking at the back of my coat, trying to pull me away. I shrugged him off.

Through the viewfinder I saw the soldiers stop.

They raised their AK 47s to their shoulders.

Then the night was split open as if a long ear-splitting roll of thunder had burst in the sky above us.

I could see it all through the viewfinder, as if I were watching under water. Long spears of flame shot out of the ends of the AK 47s. People dropped away from the crowd in the street. Some fell in heaps like sacks of grain pushed from the back of a truck. Some seemed to leap backward as if yanked on ropes, to collapse on the road, unmoving. The deafening volley continued for at least ten seconds.

The people surged away from the guns, roaring, screaming as the crowd rolled backward to the east. People around me on the sidewalk shouted in rage and terror, waving fists in the air, shrinking back towards the Great Hall a little, but not turning and running, holding on as if they were numbed by what was happening. One voice separated itself from the din. It was Lao Xu.

He had stopped pulling at my coat. 'What are they doing?' he screamed. 'What are they doing?' His face was ghostly red from the flames, his eyes wide, unbelieving.

A tiny blob of flame separated from the crowd on the sidewalk across the avenue from us, arched gracefully into the air towards the soldiers, then fell to the road, bursting and sending a miniature river of flame towards them. The snouts of the AK 47s came up in unison, spit flame, and the gunfire roared again. Bodies fell by the dozens.

Lao Xu was still screaming, in Chinese now. He pushed his way through the crowd, elbowing his way towards the soldiers. I followed him to the curb. This time it was me clutching the back of his coat.

'Lao Xu, no! Stay here!'

We had a clear view now. We were on the front rank of the people on the sidewalk. The soldiers had lowered their guns and were standing still.

Suddenly Lao Xu burst from the curb and into the street, running towards the soldiers just as they started to move forward again. He raised his hands in the air as if he imagined he could hold them back all by himself. In spite of the noise I could hear his enraged yelling.

'Ni men yi ding feng le! Ni men xiang gan shen me? Ting zhi she ji! Are you insane? What are you doing? Stop the shooting!'

'Lao Xu! Stop!' I screamed as a soldier turned towards Lao Xu's running figure.

The soldier raised his AK 47.

Crack!

Lao Xu spun around, his arms flung skyward. Before he fell the AK 47 spit flame again and the burst blew Lao Xu off his feet. His body slammed to the pavement, one leg caught under him, arms flung wide, his head twisted to the side at an impossible angle. His blood began to run onto the road, a dark stream in the red light.

Frozen, I stared at his still form. The thunder roared again. Someone beside me fell to the sidewalk. Someone fell against me, knocking me heavily to the ground on my back. Someone fell across my body, her head on my chest, facing me. There was a dark flower in the middle of her forehead. The flower slowly grew larger, then dark liquid trickled from it, flowing into her staring eye and across her cheek and onto my chest.

I shrieked and struggled, pushing her slack body away as other bodies fell around me.

The firing stopped abruptly. I got up and ran with the screaming, panicking crowd, turned the corner into Tian An Men Square, ran along the sidewalk beside the Great Hall of the People. I tripped on something and fell headlong onto the wide steps of the building. My forehead struck the concrete, sending a blinding flash of pain through my head. I got up onto my hands and knees. The fleeing crowd surged and flowed around me as I vomited on the steps.

I got to my feet, spitting and wiping my mouth on my sleeve. Strangely, the pain and convulsion of vomiting seemed to calm me a little. I looked around. The gunfire behind me had stopped. I could see that the soldiers near the burning buses had cleared a huge section of the square, the way a sharp scythe cuts down grass. There was shooting in the distance, to the south, where Eddie was.

I still had the camcorder around my wrist. I examined it, turning it over in my hands, as if I had all the time in the world. It seemed to be undamaged, although there were scuff marks on the plastic case. I raised it to my eye and videotaped the soldiers fanning out to my left.

I still had my backpack, too, so I shrugged it off and put the camcorder inside. I slung the pack back on, and took the tape recorder out of my pocket. I talked into it for a few moments, calmly, as if I were on the national news and I was reporting a bus accident in Borneo. I looked at my watch. It was 2:15 A.M. I put the recorder back in my pocket.

I know it sounds crazy, but I just sat down there on the steps and looked around. To my left, the ghostly soldiers, illuminated by the burning buses, were still slowly advancing, fanning out. I couldn't see much to the right except masses of people milling around, not sure of what to do. Directly across the square from me was the museum, lit up with amber lights. Tiny figures flitted along the edge of the roof. Tiny pin-points of light flashed, followed by the *pok-pok-pok* of the guns. Soldiers were firing down into the square. I checked out Mao's mausoleum. Soldiers lined the roof there, too. It struck me that the roof of the Great Hall behind me must be manned now, also, but still I didn't move. I sat there, numb and paralysed, calmly watching the massacre.

From behind me and to my left came the throaty rumble of diesel engines. The rumble became a roar and a grinding vibration as if a rocket was taking off right beside me. And then I saw the first tank barging into the square, slamming one of the burning buses out of its way.

The tanks came on like obscene mutant insects in science fiction movies. The orange-red light from the flames on the buses flickered across them. On the top of each tank's turret was a long machine gun. The hatches were closed.

The sight and sound of the tanks woke me up. I jumped to my feet and I ran towards the centre of the square where the students had set up their tent city. Before long I was in a mass of people again. I pushed deeper into the screaming and yelling crowd beside a line of buses.

I began to focus on faces, faces wild with anger and streaked with tears. Many of the faces were young, and many had headbands across the forehead. I was in with the students now. There were thousands of them. And they weren't moving.

I stopped. It's funny how being in the middle of a sea of bodies gives you the feeling you're safe.

I took out the two-way. 'Eddie, this is Alex. Over.'

Nothing but a low hiss answered me. I tried again. 'Eddie, can you hear me? It's Alex. Over.'

'. . . hear you . . . wrong with the radio. Over.'

'Eddie, something terrible has happened. Over.'

'. . . murdering people here, shooting indiscriminately into the crowds . . . directions . . . father? . . . – over.'

'I haven't heard from him. Over.'

Nothing but a hiss.

'Eddie! Can you hear me? Over?'

Nothing. Desperately, I switched to five.

. . . incredible. They've stopped an armoured personnel carrier and set it afire right at the back gate of Zhong Nan Hai.

. . . out of there! Get out! They're firing on the students! Repeat, they're firing on the students!

The roar of diesel engines rose in the distance. I put the radio back into my pocket and clambered onto the roof of one of the two-section buses. There were at least a dozen students up there. One was waving a huge flag of China, his body swaying with the effort. The others, men and women, stood silent and defiant, arms linked, looking towards the soldiers and the tanks. There were other buses near us, at least twenty of them, in an uneven line that didn't quite reach across the square, and on the roof of every bus was a contingent of students holding banners and waving flags.

I heard the words 'wai guo ren' and turned in the direction of the voice. A guy beside me was staring at me.

'You are American?' he asked in a thick accent. He was about my height, with long hair, a round face and wire framed glasses.

'No, Canadian.'

'Why you are here? It's very danger. You should go.'

'Why don't *you* go?'

He looked at me defiantly. 'We have made the vow to stay here as long as we must. We won't give in to fascist PLA.'

In the distance I could see the tanks beginning to fan out, facing west, and then they stopped. Tiny sparks of flame sparkled at the front of each tank a split second before we heard the roar of machine-gun fire. From around me rose shouts of anger from the students. The machine guns chattered for at least ten seconds as dozens of citizens fell, shot in the back as they ran in the direction of the Beijing Hotel.

On the bus beside the one I was on someone was shouting through a loud-hailer. I couldn't understand what she was saying. I was trying to figure out how I was going to get out of the square. There was no way I could do what Eddie wanted – get back to the hotel. Between it and me were at least a dozen tanks and hundreds of soldiers. From what Eddie had said, there were troops at the south end. The north was blocked. So that left one of the side streets. Pretty soon the square would be sealed off completely. When that happened, the soldiers might do anything, might kill all the students and citizens they could. Including me.

I had to get out of there.

But I was still my father's son. And I was still Lao Xu's friend. So I brought the camcorder to my eye and did a slow pan of the scene before me – the buses in flames, the soldiers advancing in front of the Gate of Heavenly Peace towards the Goddess of Democracy, the tanks firing.

Then, through the viewfinder, I saw the tanks, in unison, turn towards us and start to move forward. They came on, slowly, moving up on a barricade of roadway standards. The sparks flashed again. The roar of guns split the air. The tanks were advancing on the students, firing as they ground forward.

I lowered the camcorder, ready to get down off that bus. Before I had a chance to move, I saw the tanks stop. Soldiers appeared from behind them, forming in ranks, making a wide front. I scrambled down from the bus. I knew what they were going to do.

I pushed my way through the throng of students, skirting tents, bicycles, and carts. Most of the students held fast. A few moments later, the AK 47s began to rattle. And the screaming started over again.

I turned away, heading back across the square towards the Bank of China on the corner of a street that intersected with the west side of the square. Maybe I could slip down that narrow tree-lined street and get away from the tanks and the guns.

It took me about five minutes to get to the bank. I crouched behind a car in front of the bank with three or four students, trying to get my breath. The street was dark. I took off my pack again and I was putting the camcorder inside, thinking it was about time I concentrated on getting away for good, when I heard 'wai guo ren' again.

'That is TV camera?'

The woman beside me looked young. Only the dirty white headband with *Democracy Now* in Chinese on it told me she was a university student. She was short and thin, with long pigtails. Her face was streaked with dirt.

'Yes.'

'Then you are reporter. You must help us. Please tell the outside world what is happening here. You must get the news outside.'

⬛⬛⬛⬛way up onto my elbows. The move-
⬛⬛⬛⬛st the foot of the bed,
⬛⬛⬛seneck lamp on it,
⬛⬛ wardrobe of dark

She turned to the others and talked fast in Chinese. They nodded their agreement to whatever she had said. I took a look over the hood of the car. The troops in the distance had stopped firing.

Suddenly, around the corner of the bank, a squad of PLA appeared. An arrow of fear cut into my chest. I froze.

But the students behind the car with me didn't. They jumped up. Two of them, the woman and a guy with glasses on, hauled me to my feet. Their panic infected me immediately and before I knew it I was running down the dark street with them. We ran along the side of the road where the shadows were deepest.

Behind me I heard a shout, then the hollow rattle of machine-gun fire. Something that felt like a baseball bat slammed into the back of my leg, knocking it out from under me. I fell heavily to the road, face first, cracking my skull against the curb and driving all the breath from my chest. I groaned and gasped, trying to get my breath back, in a daze. I got to my knees, and tried to crawl away from the guns.

Hands pulled at my clothing, yanked my backpack off my body. Hands gripped my arms, my legs. I began to float, moaning and gasping, trying to breathe. I struggled to get free, but the iron hands held me.

I was lying on my back, on something hard. I heard voices in another language murmuring in the air around me. I lay still, drifting down into sleep, then up again to the voices and the pounding ache that filled my head, then down again. I guess I stayed half awake for quite a while. My head ached so much that I was afraid to open my eyes and my body felt so heavy, as if I was lying under a lead blanket, that I didn't want to move.

Later – I had no idea how much later – I floated up to the ache and the voices to feel a burning pain in my right leg. Slowly I opened my eyes, letting them adjust to the light. I tried to turn my head and felt an avalanche of pain thundering through my skull. I heard myself groan as I shut my eyes and kept absolutely still, hoping I would go to sleep again to stop the terrible ache. I did.

The next time I woke I felt alive at least. My head ached a bit. My leg hurt a lot. But at least my body didn't seem made of cement.

It was still light, and the first thing I thought was, what time is it? I dragged my arm from under the heavy quilt that covered me. My watch said June 4, 5:52 A.M. I thought for a second, trying to get my brain in gear. The last time I had checked my watch it was about 2:35 A.M. Add a half hour at most for what had happened in between, and I figured they got me about 3:00 A.M. So I had been out for almost three hours. It seemed more like three days.

A bolt of fear shot through me as I remembered I had been captured by soldiers. The same kind of soldiers who had murdered Lao Xu and probably grabbed my dad, or worse. The same soldiers who had shot at me. And there was no one to help me. No one else in the whole country knew where I was – or that I existed, for that matter. I was totally alone.

I heard machine-gun fire in the distance, a quick burst. The fear began to grow and spread through me, like a stain. What would they do with me? Then I remembered my backpack. When they went through it they'd find out I had been taking pictures of the PLA shooting students and citizens in Tian An Men Square. I doubted if they'd be thrilled about that.

I lay there, terrified, listening for the voices again. Or more shooting.

I found I was able to turn my head now without it pounding me with pain. Wherever I was, they had put me in a corner on a very large and very hard bed. Above me was a white plaster ceiling. The wall beside the bed was dark grey brick. On the right side of the bed there was a screen with a wood frame and green cloth panels.

Gingerly, I worked my way up onto my elbows. The movement set off the fire in my right leg. Just past the foot of the bed, against the wall, was a small desk with a gooseneck lamp on it, and beyond that what looked like a tall wardrobe of dark wood. The wall opposite me was brick to a height of about one and a half metres. The rest was window, made of square panes set into wood frames. The window was only about six metres away. In front of the window stood a wooden wash stand with a white basin on it.

I lay back down. Okay, I thought. I'm in a brick building which is six metres wide and who knows how long. I felt kind of relieved, because the furniture in the place seemed too domestic for a jail or an army barracks. I struggled up onto my right elbow and looked over the edge of the bed to the floor. It was cement, unpainted, swept very clean. I pulled the quilt back a bit. I was lying on a clean white and pink blanket. Under the blanket was a thin woven rush mattress. I peeled it back to find that I was lying on a bed made of bricks.

Lao Xu had told me about these big beds. They're called *kangs*. They're almost a metre off the floor, and they're hollow underneath so that in cold weather a fire can be set under the bed to keep the family warm. In the winter, he had told me, a Chinese family might spend a lot of time up on the *kang*.

I was starting to feel a little less terrified. I lay back and thought some more. It looked like I was in somebody's home. Okay, then. Not a modern apartment in one of the high rises of Beijing. They don't have *kangs*. I was in either one of the homes in the old *hu tong* neighbourhoods, or out in the country. The country idea seemed unlikely, so I decided I must be in a brick house in old Beijing. Either way, it looked less and less likely that I had been grabbed by soldiers.

I lay back and closed my eyes, gathering my strength to get off the bed. I heard feet brushing along the cement floor and quickly struggled up to my elbows.

Beside the bed stood an old woman. She was really short, under five feet, and very thin. She was wearing a black cotton padded jacket and trousers, like the old storyteller in the teahouse who had related the story about Zhu Ge-liang and the arrows. Her grey hair was pulled back and tied behind her neck.

Her wrinkled face lit up in a smile when she saw me and she quickly shuffled to the head of the bed and helped me sit up so

I could lean back against the wall. She tucked the quilt around me as if I were three years old, and disappeared behind the screen. In a moment she came back with a cup of tea and handed it to me.

I drank it down greedily. It wasn't too hot. The old woman stared at me while I drank, took the cup from my hands, and came back with another one. I drank all of it, too.

She took the cup away and set it on the desk. She moved carefully, the way old people sometimes do, as if they're afraid of falling down and hurting themselves. Her back was straight, though, and she looked pretty healthy to me.

She came back to the bed, smiling, pointed to my right leg, and said something. Her voice was soft, almost a whisper. She spoke again.

I nodded. My leg hurt like crazy. I pushed down the quilt and realized that I didn't have my shirt or jeans on anymore, so I pulled it up again. The old woman pretended not to notice and pulled up the bedding from the bottom of the bed.

My right calf was wrapped in strips of white cotton. Not bandages like you'd get in a hospital. Strips of cloth. I touched it carefully. At the back, above where the Achilles tendon joins the calf, a little blood had seeped through.

The old woman pulled up the quilt again and tucked me in. She brought the white enamel basin over from the washstand and set it in my lap. Then, with a soft cloth, she began to wash my face. I noticed that the water was turning pink and I wondered what my face looked like. I remembered that last night I had fallen face first onto the pavement at least twice.

When she took the basin away I closed my eyes and heaved a sigh. Well, she didn't look like PLA to me. I had no idea who she was, but I was so relieved I didn't care.

Knowing I was safe – or at least hoping I was safe – allowed me to think about other things, and the first picture that came into my mind was Lao Xu, flinging his arms into the air as the first bullets slammed into his body, then crumpling to the pavement as the second burst hit him. Then I thought about Dad. Where was he? Did the PLA have him? Then another thought hit me like

bus. The PLA had shot at me. I had a wound in my leg to prove
. Maybe they had shot at Dad. Maybe . . .

I felt overwhelmed, as if I had been swept away by a tidal
wave. I felt like I was drowning. Tears coursed down my face,
ripping off my chin onto the quilt. I brought my hands up to my
ace and let go, let the wracking sobs take me over. I cried harder
han I ever had, even harder than when Mom left us.

I heard the old woman's soothing voice beside me. She pulled
ny hands away from my face and wiped it with the cloth again.
till talking in her soft, whispery voice, she helped me lie down
nd held my hand between hers as I slipped into sleep. In the
listance, the machine guns started up again.

The next time I woke up it was just after nine o'clock. Sunlight
treamed in the window. My head felt almost normal, but my leg
till felt like there was a fire where my calf should be.

The washstand had been pulled over to the foot of the bed and
saw clothes neatly folded on the desk. I listened for the old
voman. Nothing. I threw back the quilt and got off the *kang*,
elieved to see I still had my underwear on. When I lowered
nyself to the floor and put weight on my right leg, I felt a spear of
pain jab all the way up to my hip. Using the *kang* for support, I
nopped to the desk, got the clothes, and tossed them on the bed.
Then I hopped back. I washed myself quickly, dried off with the
ittle cotton towel, and pulled on the clothes the old woman had
eft for me – a long-sleeved white shirt with a frayed collar, dark
plue baggy pants that had been mended at both knees, and a
pair of socks. The clothes were clean and pressed – and a bit too
mall for me. On the floor was a pair of cotton shoes. They fit
pretty well.

I hopped out from behind the screen to find myself in a
one-room house. It was small – you could walk across it in six or
seven strides – clean and bright. The house was square, about six
metres to the side. I looked around the sparsely furnished room.
The old woman wasn't there. The front wall had a full-length
window, except for the door in the middle of the wall.
Kitty-corner to the bed was a two-burner propane stove on metal
legs with a gas tank underneath. A big black iron *tie guo*, or wok,

sat on one burner of the stove. Next to it a small pot steamed on the other burner. Beside the stove there were shelves on the wall, the contents hidden by cloth curtains to keep out the dust. A string of garlic clumps hung from a nail driven into the end of one of the shelves. Under the shelves was a small wooden cupboard. Against the wall opposite the big window there were a small round table and four wooden chairs. Next to the edge of the screen, where I stood on one leg balancing myself, was a small black stove with a round pipe rising to the ceiling then travelling over to pass through the wall above the door.

I hopped over to the window and looked out onto a small courtyard. There were houses just like the one I was in on either side and opposite me was a high brick wall with a wide wooden door set into it. I guessed the *hu tong* was on the other side of the wall. In the middle of the courtyard, rising from the ground, was a single water pipe with a tap on it. The old woman was at the tap, filling a kettle with water.

She stood and came towards the house. I hopped to the table and lowered myself into one of the wooden chairs. When she came through the door she smiled and started to chatter away as she set down the kettle. She got out a rice bowl and filled it from the pot on the stove. She set it down in front of me, patted me on the shoulder and sat down across the table from me.

I took a pair of chopsticks from the jar on the table and attacked the steaming rice, ashamed of how hungry I felt. The rice was sort of tasteless but I didn't care. The old woman nodded encouragement as I ate, smiling and chattering away in her soft voice.

When I was halfway through the rice I stopped, embarrassed.

'*Xie xie nin*,' I said. Thank you.

She lifted a wrinkled hand and waved, as if saying goodbye. I recognized this gesture. It meant something like 'That's nothing.'

'*Bu yong xie*' she said. No need to thank. At least I think that's what she said. I couldn't pick much out of her conversation, so I figured she must be speaking some kind of dialect.

She started talking again. She must have figured I could talk Chinese because I had thanked her. I pulled my earlobe and shook my head, to show that I didn't understand.

Just when I had finished my second bowl of rice the door opened, and I was startled to see a young woman come rushing in. She was about the same age as Lan, but not as tall. I didn't recognize her at first, but it was the student I had talked to behind the car before we all ran from the PLA. She looked drawn and exhausted. Her pants and jacket were wrinkled and dirty and there was a bloodstain on her left arm.

Then everything fell into place. The students must have brought me here.

She pushed the door closed and came over to the table, saying hello to the old woman and talking quickly for a moment. The old woman shook her head sadly.

The student switched to English. 'How you are feeling?' She sat down. The old woman got up and brought her a cup of tea.

'Fine, I guess. Where am I?'

She talked English with a fairly thick accent, but I could understand everything she said. When she had to stop and think of a word she'd press her lips together and go *Mmmm*. Like this: 'Mmmm, this is our home. I, mmm, live here with my grandmother. How your leg is?'

'I don't know. I mean, it hurts a lot but I can't see how bad it is.'

Her hair was thick, parted exactly down the centre of her head, and braided. The braids were tied with elastic bands. Her moon-shaped face was sort of pretty, with strong features.

'My friend is medical student. He fixed your leg where you were shot. He says it's okay, but will be very pain for few days. He said he saw you before, in Tian An Men Square.'

Probably lots of people had, I thought. I had spent enough time there.

'Thanks,' I said, 'for helping me.'

She made the same gesture her grandmother did. Her grandmother said something.

'My grandmother asked what is your name and how old you are?'

I looked at the old woman. 'Alex. I'm seventeen.'

'Ahhh-rek-us,' said the old woman after the student had translated. Then she reached over and touched my hair.

'A friend of mine named me Shan Da,' I added, 'because my full name is Alexander.'

While the student translated, a wave of grief rolled though me. Mentioning my Chinese name made me think of Lao Xu.

'Ah, Shan Da!' The old woman nodded, pleased.

'I am Wang Xin-hua,' said the young woman. 'Wang means King or Emperor. That's the most common of the hundred Chinese surnames. Xin-hua means New China. But my grandmother calls me *Xiao Mei*. That means Little Younger Sister. You can call me by my given name, okay?'

'Okay.'

'And please call my grandmother Nai-nai. That one means –'

'Paternal Grandmother,' I cut in, remembering Teacher Huang drilling into our heads the many Chinese words for different family positions.

Xin-hua's face brightened. '*Nin hui shuo Zhong Guo hua!*'

'No, I only understand a little. I went to the school at Ri Tan Park for a couple of weeks.'

Xin-hua talked to Nai-nai for a second.

"Um, do you know what happened to my backpack?' I asked.

'Oh, yes. I get it for you.'

Xin-hua went behind the screen and brought my pack to me.

'Thanks.'

I unzipped the pack and took out all the stuff – the camcorder, tape recorder, two-way radio, and all the battery packs. I also had my map and copy of *Beijing, Old and New*. It was all there – even a couple of chocolate bars.

Nai-nai stared at the stuff as if it had just fallen off a space ship.

'You are reporter?' asked Xin-hua. I remembered that's what she had asked me last night.

I told her who I was and what I was doing in China. I told her about Dad and Lao Xu and Eddie, about Lao Xu getting killed, that I didn't know where Dad was, or Eddie either, for that matter. While I talked my throat thickened and a couple of times, as Xin-hua was translating for her grandmother, I had to work hard to keep from crying again.

Twice while I was talking we heard gunfire and we stopped and listened. Every time the machine guns sounded Xin-hua's eyes flashed angrily and Nai-nai shook her head sadly. When I had told her everything, I changed the battery in the two-way and tried to raise Eddie. No one answered.

'I will ask my friends try to find what happened to your father,' Xin-hua said.

'Thanks.'

Nai-nai got up from the table. She left the house with the washbasin and my dirty clothes while Xin-hua told me what happened after the students brought me to the house at about three o'clock that morning. She seemed really pleased when I asked her if I could tape what she said. I put fresh batteries and a new tape in the recorder and turned it on.

When Xin-hua and her friends had met up with me they were returning to the square after taking some wounded people on the back of a pedicab to a nearby hospital. Ambulances had a tough time getting near the square because the PLA wouldn't let them by. The corridors of the hospital were already jammed with wounded, dying, and dead when they got there.

Once they had taken me to the house – they didn't want to take me to the hospital because the PLA had already begun to hunt foreign journalists – they went back to the square. Xin-hua's house was south of the square, off Qian Men Street.

Even though the PLA was vicious in its attacks on the citizens in and around the square, people just wouldn't give up. And they wouldn't go away. They pushed buses across streets and torched them. They threw bottles and stones and molotov cocktails at the soldiers, ran like the wind when the shooting started up, then returned when the shooting died away. In the square, the soldiers mowed down hundreds and hundreds of unarmed people. Every five or ten minutes the loudspeakers on the streetlight poles blared messages urging people to 'stop chaos' and go home. At four o'clock the lights in the square went out, plunging the thousands of citizens and students into complete darkness except ˙he hellish glow of the burning vehicles. Everyone got ready ˡl-out attack. But not much changed. Forty minutes later came back on. By then the PLA had completely ..... the square.

They ordered the students to clear the square or face the consequences, as if they hadn't been doing that for hours.

Xin-hua and her friends had joined their contingent from *Ren Min Da Xue*, People's University. The student leaders had a meeting and decided to do as the PLA asked, but when they reported to their various groups, a few hundred students refused to leave. They wanted to offer passive resistance to the PLA.

Walking arm in arm, Xin-hua and the other thousands of students slowly filed out of the square to the south. They were beaten with truncheons by police as they left. Behind them they heard the AK 47s open fire. They knew the friends and classmates who had stayed were being massacred where they stood.

Many of them circled around to the north and west, entering Chang An Avenue and moving east again. They got as far as the Beijing Hotel, where masses of citizens and students were surging towards them, getting shot at, then fleeing east, like an enraged tidal flow.

Not long after the gunfire in the square dwindled, bonfires began to appear.

'Bonfires?' I interrupted her.

'Yes. At first we didn't know what those were. Later we heard that PLA were burning the bodies.'

She stopped talking. She was weeping quietly. I swallowed hard.

Burning the bodies.

'Why would they do that?' I finally choked out.

'Because they will say that it didn't happen. That they didn't kill anyone.'

I let that go. Obviously Xin-hua was so overcome with grief and fear and outrage that she wasn't being sensible. Nobody, I thought, could possibly deny what the PLA was doing.

I felt angrier than I ever have. 'Nobody will be able to pretend this isn't happening,' I vowed, 'because I've got it on tape. And I'm going to see that the tapes, somehow, get back to Canada.'

Xin-hua looked straight into my eyes. 'That is what we are hoping, Shan Da.'

I suddenly had a thought. 'Hey, wait! Maybe the Americans are still on the radio!'

I shut off the recorder and grabbed the two-way. I switched to five.

The Americans were still at their stations – except for the one who had been in the square and she was back at the Beijing Hotel. As soon as I raised them I asked about my dad, but they knew nothing yet, about him or Eddie.

For the rest of that day Xin-hua and I monitored the Americans, using the tape recorder and making notes. All morning the chaos in the streets continued. There was still lots of action right in front of the hotel. By ten o'clock there were at least twenty bodies in the street. The soldiers were even firing on people who came in to get the wounded.

Around lunchtime three of Xin-hua's friends came by. They looked bedraggled and exhausted. As soon as they came in I knew who had bandaged my leg.

'Hong!' I blurted.

All four of them stared at me like I'd lost my mind. Xin-hua introduced them – Yang, Liu and Nie. Nie was the guy in the red baseball cap I had talked to in the square.

'How is your friend?' I asked him. I was smart enough not to call her Lan.

'She is home from hospital now,' he said. 'I am okay, too.'

The students sat down and they all started talking at once – passing on the latest news and rumours, I guessed. At one point

Xin-hua turned to me and said sadly, 'PLA have torn down the Goddess of Democracy.'

After the gabble wound down the guys hooked in to the two-way and listened carefully while Xiao Nie unwrapped my bandages, washed out the wound, and redressed it. The bullet had gouged out a bloody trench in my calf about the size of my thumb. I wondered if I'd ever be able to walk normally again.

I asked Xiao Nie where the bathroom was. After outfitting me with a hat and sunglasses to hide my foreignness he took me outside and we hobbled through the courtyard, me with my arm around his shoulders. I looked around but I couldn't see any kind of outhouse. Xiao Nie took me to the door in the wall – the Chinese call it a 'gate', too – and helped me through. Overhead we heard the *whok-whok-whok-whok* of a helicopter. We struggled along the *hu tong* for a few minutes. The pain in my head was so bad I kept my head down and held my eyes clamped shut most of the time. Finally we stopped outside a small brick building. You could tell long before you got to it that it was a public bathroom. I read the big character meaning male painted on the brick.

We got back to the house to find that Nai-nai had made us a lunch of noodles and everybody slurped and chewed away. After lunch the three guys left.

The war in the streets went on all afternoon and into the early evening. By nightfall the square was full of tanks and from what we could gather – the Americans had stopped transmitting – the only people left there were soldiers.

Xin-hua woke me up around ten. I had laid my head on my arms at the table to rest for a second and had fallen straight to sleep.

'Go to bed now, Shan Da.'

A small cot had been made up between the table and the screen. Xin-hua disappeared behind the screen after saying good night, leaving me a flashlight and turning off the single overhead light. I hopped to the cot, carefully lowered myself down and struggled out of my clothes.

I lay back and switched off the flashlight. As I stared into the dark, gunfire sounded in the distance, like murderous firecrackers. The citizens were still fighting in the streets. The soldiers were still killing them. But as I lay there I had only one thought. When would it end, so I could go out and start looking for my dad?

六月六日

June 6

I spent the fifth hobbling and moping around, wearing out batteries on the two-way trying to raise somebody, lying down when my head and leg shouted too loud at me, sleeping fitfully. The sky was overcast and the big wind swirled dust devils around the courtyard.

I took a look at myself in a little mirror in the corner near the washstand. My nose was one big red scab, one eye had an ugly yellow circle around it, and my chin was scraped.

Xin-hua was nowhere to be seen. Nai-nai drifted around doing housework, cooking, going out and in the door. I got in her way a lot, but she was smiling and polite and worried-looking. I felt grumpy and frustrated and scared.

I woke up at six the next morning. A few seconds after I opened my eyes I wished I hadn't wakened at all. I groaned. My wound hurt so much I could hardly move it.

Xin-hua and Nai-nai were up already. Nai-nai was at the stove, filling one of the big thermoses from the kettle. Xin-hua sat at the table, as if she'd been there all night. She was dressed in clean clothes now, grey slacks and a yellow shirt.

She must have heard me groan. She looked up at me and said good morning.

'Hi,' I managed, wondering how I was going to get out of bed and dress with her a few feet away from me.

As if reading my mind, Xin-hua said something to her grandmother and the both of them lifted the screen into place between me and the table. I struggled to a sitting position and pulled on my pants and socks, then balanced on my left leg and put on the shirt. After slipping on my shoes I hopped out from around the screen and plopped down into one of the chairs.

I must have winced, because Xin-hua asked, 'Your leg is more worse?'

I nodded.

'Give you these. Xiao Nie left them for you,' she said, handing me two white pills.

Nai-nai brought me a cup of hot water and I swallowed the pills.

Xin-hua was fiddling with the dial of a radio I hadn't seen yesterday.

'Shortwave?'

'Yes. This morning before it got light I back to my university to get some things. My classmate told me government is stopping Voice of America and BBC. I can't get those.'

'Jamming,' I said.

'What?'

'It's called jamming'. I remembered what Xin-hua had said the day before yesterday about the PLA burning the bodies of the people they had shot in the square. Destroying the evidence. 'The government must be jamming the shortwave broadcasts from abroad so the truth doesn't get in.'

Xin-hua nodded. It's kind of crazy, I thought to myself. The news gets *out* of China through foreigners smuggling out videos, giving eyewitness accounts when they get to Hong Kong or Tokyo or San Francisco, or just making long distance phone calls, then the news comes back *in* again on shortwave. Did Deng and Li and the gang really think they could stop it? I looked at all the electronic gear on the table – battery packs, two-way radio, video and audio recorders, the shortwave. What kind of world did those guys think they were living in, anyway?

The radio was a Chinese model and was plugged into the light socket above the table. It hissed and sputtered, then shouted Chinese, then hissed some more as Xin-hua turned the dial. Finally she shut it off.

I turned on the two-way and called over five. 'Hello. Anybody there? Over.'

I tried three or four times on all the channels but got nothing. I switched back to five and left the set on.

Nai-nai brought a bowl of rice gruel to me. I nodded my thanks and she went out into the courtyard. The gruel steamed up into my face. The steam felt so good on my scraped skin I held my face over the bowl for a moment. When I had slurped the last grains out of the bowl Xin-hua got up and went to the desk. She brought back a black lacquered cane.

'This was my grandfather's,' she said. 'Nai-nai said you should use it.'

'Great,' I said, and pulled myself up. I tried out the cane, hobbling around the house. It was hard to use because if I wasn't careful I lost my balance when I stepped onto my good leg, but it sure was better than hopping. My headache was pretty mild that morning, or maybe it only seemed that way because my leg hurt so much.

I got my hat and sunglasses and struggled outside to use the tap to wash my face. Nai-nai was bent over a wash tub, both sleeves pushed up to her elbows, washing clothes on a wooden washboard. I recognized the shirt she was grinding up and down on the washboard. It was mine. There were two women with her, sitting on either side of her on low stools. One was washing rice and the other was doing something with some celery. Both women were grey haired. One was a little bit chubby, the other as thin as Nai-nai, but taller. The larger woman was dressed in black but the other was wearing blue slacks and a white shirt.

As soon as they saw me they broke into a storm of gabble and got to their feet. They approached me smiling and talking to Nai-nai as if I wasn't really there. Both of them touched my hair as they talked. I figured that they were treating me like a post with blonde hair and blue eyes because they thought I couldn't talk Chinese, so I said hello to them.

They laughed, surprised that words they understood came out of my mouth. The thin one pointed to my leg. '*Nin shen ti hao bu hao?*' she asked. Is your health good?

'*Zhe ge bu hao,*' I told her, pointing to my leg. Even the walk from the house had increased the pain.

While they jabbered away – I could pick out quite a few of their words, so I guessed they were Beijingese – I bent and washed my face at the tap and tried to clean my teeth with my finger. Half the courtyard was in shadow because the sun hadn't climbed high enough to throw its rays over the wall yet. The houses on either side seemed to be identical to Nai-nai's house. Each one had a bike leaning against it. The courtyard was swept so clean you could have found a button in two seconds. I liked the courtyard. It was private, quiet – except for the chattering of the three women, who were back to work – and peaceful. I felt safe there because of the wall between the yard and the alley.

I hobbled towards the wooden door and carefully negotiated my way into the *hu tong*. It was already pretty hot out. I made my way along the curved alley. It was about the width of one and a half cars, with high walls on both sides, naturally, and a sort of asphalt surface. It was swept clean, too.

I passed an old woman pushing a bamboo baby carriage, keeping my head down. She nodded to me. Nearer the public bathroom a couple of kids wearing monkey masks were play fighting with staves.

On my way back to Nai-nai's gate I heard someone talking through a loud-hailer. His words bounced and echoed down the canyon of the *hu tong*. I made my painful way past the gate, continuing around the curve for about twenty meters to where the alley straightened out. Just along from there was an intersection. Someone was selling Chinese celery from the back of one of those vehicles that looked like a giant tricycle with a flat platform behind the rider – a *ping ban che*. On the opposite corner an old man squatted next to a carefully stacked pile of round watermelons. Beside the *ping ban che* about two dozen people had gathered around a young man who stood astride a bike. He was talking to them through the loud-hailer. He stopped when machine-gun fire popped rapidly in the distance, then started up again. When he finished, he mounted the bike and rode off.

When I got back to the house I asked Xin-hua if she knew what that guy might have been doing. She told me that the young man was probably a news spreader. People like him were going around the city, passing on the latest news at a free market or *hu tong* corner, then riding on to the next spot. I knew that what they were doing was illegal, what Lao Xu had called 'spreading rumours', and that if they were caught they'd be in big trouble. Maybe even be shot.

'We have no other way to find out what is happening,' she said. 'Only one radio station now and it is all lies. Same thing with TV.'

I had to lie down. My leg was killing me and my headache was worse. My cot had been folded up and put away so Xin-hua helped me up onto the *kang*. She brought me a couple more of the pills. I swallowed them and lay back.

I felt trapped and totally frustrated and sick with worry about my dad. Maybe, I thought, maybe I should just walk along the *hu tong* until I got to a main street and hail a cab or get on a bus or something. One thing was sure, I couldn't walk or take a bicycle. But I could make it to the Beijing Hotel *some*how.

But between me and the hotel was Tian An Men Square, which was now full of tanks and PLA.

Well, maybe I could skirt the square, just take a long way

around. Then I remembered. There were barricades on all the roads leading to the square. And in other places, all over the city. Maybe buses weren't running yet. Maybe taxis weren't either. I wondered if I could get Xin-hua to help me back to the hotel.

My thoughts were interrupted by a long burst of AK 47 fire, then a couple of short bursts. I flinched, feeling suddenly afraid. Maybe it wasn't so safe for anybody to be out on the main streets, I thought.

After lunch – noodles again – Xin-hua's friends came by. I was up again, not because I felt any better but because it was too depressing lying on the bed behind the screen.

Xiao Nie immediately examined my leg. He rolled up the pant leg and slowly unwound the bandage while the others watched. It stung like mad because the dried blood had glued the bandage and my leg hairs and the skin all together. I felt stupid, trying not to howl in the presence of three people who had been shot at a couple of days ago. By the time bandage was off I was breathing hard and blinking hard, hoping no one noticed I was about to faint. I twisted my leg a bit and looked at the wound. It was all dark red with old blood and sort of an ugly yellow colour tinged the muscle around it. There was still a fair amount of swelling, too.

'It's better,' Xiao Nie said.

'It feels worse.'

'That mean it's healing.'

He said something in Chinese and Xiao Yang, a small guy with thick horn-rimmed glasses handed him a small green canvas bag. Xiao Nie rummaged around inside and came out with a paper packet. He unfolded it and sprinkled some white powder on the wound. Then he reached into his shirt pocket and drew out two little paper envelopes.

Putting them on the table beside the hissing two-way radio he said, 'Take these. One from each package every four hours.'

'What are they?' I was imagining some ancient Chinese medicine like eye of newt or powdered tiger's teeth or something.

'One is painkiller. The another one is tetracycline, antibiotic.

Now I give you this treatment.'

From his little green bag Xiao Nie removed a clear plastic sack with a lot of different-length needles in it and a bottle of clear liquid. 'Needles for the acupuncture,' he explained. 'It will ease your pain and help the swell to go away.'

'Acupuncture? Are you kidding?' I wasn't too fussy about the idea of anyone sticking needles into me. I couldn't believe a real doctor was using voodoo stuff like that.

'I thought you went to the western-style medical college,' I said to Xiao Nie. In China there are also traditional medical colleges where you can go and learn about roots and berries and needles.

'Yes, Shan Da. Acupuncture is good. Many of Western doctors are using it.'

Maybe so, but not on me, I thought. My leg didn't agree with me. As soon as Xiao Nie finished his sentence, a firecracker of pain flared in my wound.

'Does it hurt?'

'Little bit of pain, but goes away fast.'

'Okay, try it,' I said. What did I have to lose? 'But if I say stop, stop. Okay?'

'Very okay, Shan Da.'

Xiao Nie sat down across from me – which surprised me. How was he going to stick needles in my leg from his chair? He took the needles from the little plastic bag and spread them out. Then he unscrewed the cap of the bottle.

'Give me your left hand, please, Shan Da.'

I did as he asked, curious. He turned my hand palm down on the table and took my wrist, feeling around with his thumb where hand and wrist met. He seemed to find a spot he liked. Holding my arm firmly, he chose a needle, about ten centimetres long and dipped the point into the liquid. I guessed that was to sterilize it.

He put the needle against my skin where his thumb had been and pushed it into my wrist. It stung like it does when – well, when you're getting a needle. He twirled the needle slowly clockwise, then counterclockwise. The sting went away.

Within a few minutes he had placed three needles around the first one. He looked up and smiled. 'Any paining, Shan Da?'

'No. Nothing.' I stared at the needles. Okay, I thought, now my wrist looks like I had an argument with a porcupine, but what's my wrist got to do with a bullet wound in my calf?

'Xiao Nie, why are you putting the needles in *there*?'

'Send your *qi* over to your hurt spot, Shan Da.'

'Oh.' I didn't have the faintest idea what he was talking about. I watched as he put three more needles into the back of my hand. Then he knelt in front of me.

'Those needles for healing. Now I put some to make the swell go away.'

Xiao Nie inserted a couple of needles below the wound and a couple above it, twirling each one before letting it go. He stood up and screwed the cap back onto the bottle.

While I sat there, punctured, Xin-hua's friends passed on the news and rumours they'd picked up. Xiao Nie was helping out when he could at the Union Hospital. Xiao Yang had been touring on his bike, secretly taking pictures. He put two rolls of exposed film on the table. I wondered why, but didn't say anything. Xiao Liu, a big solid guy who made Xin-hua and Xiao Yang look like kindergarten kids beside him, had been checking out the university campuses because most students thought that it was only a matter of time before the PLA raided the campuses. They were afraid of another bloodbath.

They talked in Chinese – Xiao Liu had no English because his foreign language was Japanese – and Xin-hua would stop every few minutes and translate for me as best she could with her limited vocabulary. Probably she didn't have words like *murder, blood, bullet, tank,* and *armoured personnel carrier* in her English textbooks. While she talked to me I made notes, then when she switched to Chinese with her friends, I put a summary on the tape recorder. I had to do it that way because I was starting to run low on tapes.

This is what they found out.

The Chinese Red Cross estimated 2,600 civilians and students dead so far.

Police were patrolling the city in groups with iron truncheons. The PLA were at most of the intersections and doing spot checks, demanding to see people's identity papers. PLA in plain clothes with heavy canvas shoulder bags were patrolling the city. There were machine guns in the bags. Were the PLA using the civilians for cover for some reason?

In many neighbourhoods, life goes on as usual. People are shopping, sitting in the shade of the plane trees, playing with their kids.

On a side street out near the Friendship Hotel a truck full of soldiers was moving slowly along because the street was narrow. A street sweeper threw down his broom and lay on the pavement in front of the truck to prevent it going forward. He was arrested.

PLA forced their way into the Capital Hospital and arrested a camera crew who were taking pictures of the wounded. Doctors had let them in against strict orders. Two doctors were shot.

Outside the Citi building soldiers pulled a man off a bicycle and beat him with the butts of their AK 47s. 'I have a wife! I have a wife!' he yelled as they struck him. At the same place soldiers rounded up civilians from the street and forced them to kneel with guns at the back of their necks for forty minutes, then let them go.

There are rumours that the soldiers of the Twenty-seventh army have been fired upon by other troops because of what had happened at the square. Also that, on the night of the massacre, soldiers from the Twenty-seventh Army stood behind other troops and shot them if they refused to fire on the students.

In the east part of the city, near the Workers' Gymnasium, a truckload of soldiers rumbled down a residential street. An old lady standing on her fourth-storey balcony shouted at them, waving her fist, '*Fa xi shi! Fa xi shi!*' Fascists! Fascists! She was shot from the moving truck and she toppled over the balcony railing into the street.

Tanks are massed ten across and eight deep at the north end of Tian An Men Square. There are three hundred thousand PLA in and around Beijing. Tanks are deployed at strategic spots, like major intersections of the Second Ring Road. The big diplomatic residence compound on the Second Ring Road has been ordered evacuated. I looked up when Xin-hua told me that, remembering the map of Beijing in my head, remembering when I showed Eddie and Dad where I thought the PLA would enter the city. The tanks set up in that way meant only one thing – whoever deployed the tanks was expecting an attack. It seemed Beijing was on the verge of civil war.

June 7

Today was What To Do With Alex Day. Or, I should say, With Shan Da.

It was pretty much like yesterday – sunny and hot, with no breeze to stir the poplars in the courtyard. I couldn't move around too much. I guess I had overdone things yesterday, tried to hurry the wound along. Today I paid for it. The wound raged and complained and every move I made sent a fiery bolt right up to my knee.

So I sat around and got in Nai-nai's way all day.

I was really on edge. Nothing on the two-way, nothing to do

except sit or lie around feeling sore in the head and leg, wondering when and how I was going to get out of this place, thinking about Lao Xu, worrying about Dad, wondering what had happened to Eddie the night of the massacre – in other words, I was going nuts with frustration.

On the top of that, I was homesick. I missed my friends. I wanted to be in my own room in my own house. And I wanted Dad there with me.

Tears ran from the corners of my eyes, hot and ticklish. I took a deep breath to stop the crying and let it out slow.

I decided that no matter how badly my leg hurt and no matter what Nai-nai or Xin-hua thought, I was going to leave tomorrow morning. I would thank them for taking care of me and I would ask to borrow the cane. I would make my way along the *hu tong* until I got to a major street. Then I would try to get back to the hotel. I knew I was south of the square, and as long as it was still sunny, I'd be able to figure out where north was.

If I met soldiers, well, I'd have to try my luck.

I felt a little better after I had made my decision, and I dozed off and slept till suppertime.

Our meal was boiled rice and stir-fried celery with soya bean sauce and sugar in it. That's it. A typical meal, Xin-hua told me. Not much like the Beijing Hotel. I realized that the meals there and in the Chinese restaurants in Toronto don't have much to do with what people actually eat in China.

After supper, Xiao Nie and Xiao Yang came by. They looked tired and scared and sad at the same time. But I had never known them when they *didn't* look that way.

Right away I asked them if they had heard anything about my father. Xiao Nie didn't say anything. He dropped his canvas bag on the table, then knelt and began to unwrap my bandage, keeping his head down as he worked. Xin-hua and Xiao Yang rattled away in Chinese and every few seconds Xin-hua looked across the table at me, her face anxious.

'What?' I interrupted. 'What?'

They kept talking fast. I couldn't follow even one word.

'Is it about my father? Did they hear anything?'

Xiao Yang fell silent. Xin-hua said, 'No, nothing your father. But Xiao Liu has been back to Harbin. He heard that some students are being arrested.'

'Will he be okay?'

'We don't know. Hope he will. This afternoon a BBC reporter was found on streets by PLA. They beat him and made him to kneel down on street with the gun on his neck.'

'Did they let him go?'

'They arrested him. Xiao Yang thinks those arrested are driven out.'

'Out of the country?'

'Perhaps.'

That didn't sound so bad to me, if it was true. It would have suited me just fine to let them take me to the airport and put me on a plane to anywhere else.

Then I thought about Dad. Had he been driven out? What if I spent days looking for him and he was out of the country all along? But Dad would never let them evacuate him unless he knew where I was.

I had to get to the Beijing Hotel. He or Eddie might be there. And if they weren't, the suite would still be the place to start looking. I needed my passport and some money. And, I thought to myself, there might still be some foreign correspondents who hadn't left yet. They might know something. And even if they didn't, they could help me.

Xiao Yang and Xin-hua were talking again. 'Foreigners are fleeing Beijing,' she said. 'Embassies are telling their people to leave. Everyone is afraid of the civil war.'

'Xin-hua, I want to leave. Now. Right away.'

'Yes,' she answered, then ignored me and started talking to Xiao Yang again. Xiao Nie got up from his knees. I had paid no attention while he was redressing my leg. He sat down, drew two of the tiny envelopes out of his pocket, and gave them to me. He joined in on the conversation.

The talk was rapid, but I caught on after a few minutes that I was the topic. It was really frustrating, sitting there listening to them, looking from face to face. I interrupted a couple of times, but Xiao Nie and Xin-hua said to wait a bit. I didn't want to wait a bit. And I didn't want to sit there being talked about like a bundle of celery. I knew what I wanted to do.

Nai-nai joined in, too. She prepared some tea, tossing her own opinions over her shoulder as she stood at the stove.

I gave up waiting for Xin-hua to tell me what the big discussion was producing. I got my pack and took out my map of Beijing. I spread it out on the table, intending to plan my route to the hotel.

I tapped Xin-hua on the arm and interrupted. 'Xin-hua, where are we exactly?'

'*Ah, ta you di tu,*' exclaimed Xiao Yang. 'He has a map!' And he snatched the map, turned it around and started talking again. Xiao Nie rose from his chair and leaned over the map. Xin-hua got up on both knees and leaned one elbow on the table. Their fingers darted all over the place, and every few seconds one would turn the map and stab it a few times with a fingertip.

I gave up completely. Let them talk, I thought. I knew what I was going to do.

Nai-nai put a cup of tea down in front of me. I said thanks and added, '*Wo de yi fu zai nar?*' That was as close as I could get to Where are my clothes?

She went to the tall wardrobe and lifted down my neatly folded clothes. She brought them over and put them on the table.

Xin-hua saw them and said something to Nai-nai that began with *Bu*, No, picking up the clothes and handing them back to her. Nai-nai returned the clothes to the wardrobe and shut the door.

'Hey!' I yelled. 'Wait just a minute!'

The three university students fell silent. 'I want my clothes,' I said, taking advantage of the lull. 'I'm leaving tomorrow. For sure.'

'Wait a bit, Shan Da,' Xin-hua said. 'We are discussing your case.'

'Yeah, well, how about letting *me* in on the discussion of my case.'

'Please wait. We are trying to decide what to do.' And off they went again.

I sat back and let them go at it. Forget it, I thought for the tenth time, let them talk. Tomorrow I would do what I wanted.

While I watched them, detached now, it soon became clear that Xin-hua was the leader of the group. Funny how I had never noticed it before. She dominated the discussion. She'd say something, stabbing the map or shaking her open hand to make a point, then one or both of the other guys would respond, as if testing their own ideas against what she had said. Then she'd talk again and they'd nod. Then all three would talk at once.

I busied myself putting all my stuff into my pack – all except the two-way, which I left on, as usual. All that day I had been monitoring every channel, leaving it on one channel for ten minutes so, then switching to the next. That way I covered all channels at least once an hour. But all I got all day was a low hiss.

I was zipping up the pack when I noticed that the talk had stopped.

'Shan Da,' Xin-hua began, 'we want to ask you something.'

'What?'

'We want you try take all your materials – tapes and notes – outside.'

'Outside?' What was she talking about? Then it dawned on me. She meant outside the country.

'Sure,' I said. 'I would have done that anyway.'

She said something to the others. They nodded. Xiao Nie talked to Xin-hua for a second.

She nodded and said, 'We want you know that's very dangerous. If PLA or Public Security Bureau finds that stuffs, you will get very big trouble. Maybe arrested.' She cleared her throat. 'Maybe shot.'

When she said that, it was like someone had bashed me on the back of the head with a board. I hadn't really considered *not* taking the videos with me. I had assumed I would, because, before and during the night of the fourth, I had a blind urge to make sure I kept a record of everything. I wanted to do it for Dad. And for Lao Xu.

But what about now? Things had changed. And maybe my attitude had changed. Getting shot will change anybody's attitude. What I wanted most was to get out of China, to leave the horror behind me. I didn't care anymore. I just wanted to go home. China wasn't my country. I wasn't responsible for what happened. I didn't even understand it. So why should I risk my neck? What was in it for me, except maybe a bullet in the back of the head?

'We have a plan,' Xin-hua went on. 'I will take you to Canada Embassy. Xiao Nie says the foreigners are going to their embassies, then outside.'

She turned the map so I could read it and put her finger on a spot far on the eastern side of the city. 'Here on San Li Tun Street is Canada Embassy. It's far from here – this is here – but we can make it in one day.'

'I can't walk that far,' I said. I was stalling for time so I could think about things more.

'I will take you on back of *ping ban che*.'

'But I think I should go back to the Beijing Hotel first. My father might be there. I can talk to the other reporters and ask them if they know anything.'

A burst of talk. I guessed both Xiao Nie and Xiao Yang picked up on the words Beijing Hotel.

'That's very too dangerous, Shan Da. Too many PLA around there.'

'But they wouldn't stop me. I'm a foreigner. I'm staying there.'

'They would stop you and search you, Shan Da, before getting there. You have no passport with you. And you have the camera and the films.'

'What if I didn't have the camera and films?'

A flicker of disappointment crossed her face. 'We still think that's too dangerous. Much better to go right to embassy. They will know the news about your father.'

'I'd still like to go to the hotel first. My dad might be waiting there for me.'

Xin-hua talked to the others for a minute. Xiao Nie and Xiao Yang shook their heads. Xin-hua turned to me, about to speak when Xiao Yang grabbed her arm and said something angrily and hit the table with the flat of his hand. That set the three of them off on another long round of talking.

I couldn't stand it anymore. I struggled to my feet, grabbed my cane, and went outside. It was dark in the courtyard. Dark and quiet. Someone had left a low stool by the water tap, and I hobbled over and carefully lowered myself onto it.

I heard machine-gun fire a long way off in the night, a short burst that sent a pang of fear through me. I tried to get my spinning thoughts into some kind of order.

Probably Xin-hua was right about not going back to the hotel. If the embassies were pulling their nationals out of the country and if Dad was not in jail, they had probably got in touch with him. But I couldn't see him going anywhere without me. He certainly wouldn't leave China. So the question was, would he leave the hotel and go to the embassy or the airport? I tried to think the way he would. Maybe he'd think the best place to find me was at the embassy. He knew how familiar I was with the city.

I shook my head, trying to clear it, and pounded the hard earth of the courtyard in frustration. What would *he* do?

Okay, the embassy, I decided. If Dad wasn't there, then the staff could help me find him better than I could on my own. If the phones were still working, they could call him. Yes, that made sense. I'd go to the embassy.

A single gunshot sounded, closer this time. I flinched again and the sudden movement sent a jolt of pain through my leg.

Next decision. What about Xin-hua's request? I figured I'd tell her no. I'd leave the stuff with her and if she wanted to try to get it smuggled out of the country she was welcome. I had already been shot once, and I wasn't sure how I'd act when I saw another PLA and his AK 47 with a bayonet sticking up from the barrel. What I did know was that the thought of being shot at again terrified me. So did the idea of rotting in a Chinese prison.

I heaved a big sigh and looked up at the piece of moon shining through the poplar leaves overhead. The night was still and warm and peaceful. Except for the gunfire.

I was trying to decide how I'd tell Xin-hua I'd made up my mind to leave the tapes and stuff with her, when I caught sight of a bicycle leaning against the house on the right of the courtyard. Faint light from the big front window played along the bike's frame and illuminated the spokes with a soft glow. I shuddered. I remembered seeing three or four bikes near one of the barricades in Tian An Men Square. An armoured personnel carrier had run up and over the barricade and was stopped, burning, on the other side. It had run over and crushed the bikes. I hadn't been able to see them at the time, but I knew that for each mangled bike there was a dead body lying on the pavement of the square in the dark, and that the big tires of the personnel carrier were wet with blood. What kind of monster would run over unarmed civilians with one of those huge powerful machines and grind their bodies into the pavement? Or shoot into the backs of fleeing men and women?

Lao Xu's body had lain on the pavement of Chang An Avenue, torn open by machine-gun bullets. Was it still there? Had the PLA taken his body and thrown it onto a pile of other bodies and set fire to it? The horrible image of human beings burning like fallen branches pushed all the fear out of my mind and replaced it with searing anger.

Just as quickly, I felt shame. So much shame that a hot blush swelled up my body and neck and into my face.

I looked back into the house. Xin-hua and Xiao Nie and Xiao Yang were still talking, still gesticulating. They had saved my life. Xin-hua had brought me to her home. Xiao Nie had taken care of my injuries. Xiao Yang had scoured the city for news of my father. Nai-nai had allowed me to stay in her home, and for the first time it struck me that if the PLA discovered me there, all four of them would be shot as traitors.

I jabbed the cane into the dirt and pulled myself to my feet, knocking over the little stool. I hobbled as quickly as I could to the door and shoved it open. The talking stopped.

'We're going to the embassy,' I said to Xin-hua, 'and we're

taking the videos and the audio tapes and my notes with us. And,
I added, 'we're going to take *more* pictures along the way!'

We spent the next few hours getting ready. I wanted to leave right
away, but there were two good reasons why we couldn't. First,
Xiao Yang had to go back home and get his dad's *ping ban che*.
Second, under martial law there's a curfew. Xin-hua and the
others thought that travelling at night would be even more
dangerous than in the daytime, especially when they considered
the plan they had.

The plan was that Xin-hua and I would be transporting a new
Peony washing machine through the city on the back of the *ping
ban che*. It was a great idea. I liked it as soon as I heard it. In
Beijing, a lot of people were buying new refrigerators and washers
from the Chinese factories that had recently been set up by
Japanese companies. Very few people up till now have had
fridges or electric washers. *Nobody* had automatic dryers.
Anyway, when people were able to get one of these new status
symbols, which were in short supply, he or she usually hired
someone with a *ping ban che* to transport the thing home. Every
day I saw them in the city, tied carefully to the back of the *che*,
with a proud and anxious owner often riding on the platform
beside the new machine.

Xin-hua would be the delivery woman and I would be the
helper. That way I could ride on the back, lying down and taking
it easy like any worker who wasn't strictly on duty until the
destination had been reached. Xiao Yang's dad had just bought a
washer himself, so Xiao Yang was going back home to get the *che*
and the empty box.

I figured I could rig up the camcorder something like the way I
did on my bike. We could turn it on anytime we wanted and tape
anything we passed.

So, while Xiao Yang was out, I got all my gear ready. After a
big discussion in Chinese that I wasn't allowed to join in on, it was
decided that we would leave the two-way and the audio recorder

behind because we wouldn't need them. Xiao Yang would get rid of them later. It was also decided that I would wear the clothes I had on, rather than my own, because mine looked too new and not Chinese enough. Nai-nai found me a hat in the wardrobe.

The next step in the plan I wasn't too thrilled with. Xin-hua said that she wanted to dye my hair black.

'Sunglass will hide your blue eyes,' she said, 'but your hair does not look Chinese.'

So, while Xiao Nie put together a little first-aid kit for us in case my leg started to bleed again, Xin-hua dyed my hair. With black shoe polish.

The polish had an evil smell and felt like someone had gobbed about a pound of margarine on my head. Xin-hua combed and combed, and gradually I changed from a blonde to a dark-haired worker. When she was finished I looked in the mirror and figured that if the shoe polish ever dried and if I pulled the hat down far enough, I might get away with it.

When Xiao Yang got back I rigged up the camcorder. What I did was, I made a sort of cradle out of coat hangers so that the camera could be suspended inside the cardboard carton with the lens peeping through a small hole that I cut out right in the centre of one of the Peony logos. We put some broken bricks in the bottom to give the box stability.

By three in the morning we were ready. Nobody could sleep, so we sat around drinking tea until dawn came. On my map Xin-hua showed me the route she was planning to take to the embassy. It was basically a big circle to the west and north, then back across the top of the city. The embassy was on the east side of the city.

'We shouldn't go this way,' she said, indicating the area east of her neighbourhood. 'Too many PLA around the train station. This part of Beijing I don't know very well. But I know the city quite well the way we will go.'

So we waited for the dawn. I was glad I was finally *doing* something. I wish I could say I was filled with breathless anticipation. I wasn't. My stomach was knotted with fear and I kept wondering if I was making a foolish mistake.

六月八日

June 8

The morning dawned warm, muggy, and overcast. The leaves on the poplars in the courtyard hung limp in the still air.

Xiao Yang was outside checking the *che* over for the thousandth time. Nai-nai was putting some rice and pickled vegetables into two metal boxes, pressing the boiled rice down with a big spoon. She put on the lids and put the boxes into Xin-hua's canvas shoulder bag along with the first-aid kit. She added a bottle of boiled water.

I put on my jacket, which I was sure I wouldn't need on such a muggy day, but the committee – Xin-hua, Xiao Nie, and Xiao

Yang – insisted. I was relieved to see that the shoe polish had dried, but it left my hair stiff. I pulled my hat down as far as it would go. In the mirror I saw a strange creature with very unconvincing black hair, blue eyes, and a scratched up face with a long scab down his nose.

I had no headache that morning but my leg was stiff and sore. I gimped my way over to the table and slung on my backpack.

Xiao Nie and Xiao Yang had gone outside. I hobbled to the wardrobe where Nai-nai was rummaging around and, with my weight on my left leg, leaned the cane up against the wardrobe. I grabbed her hand and held it in both of mine, shaking it slowly and gently.

'*Xie xie nin*,' I said. '*Ma fan nin le.*' Thank you. I cause you a lot of trouble. Somehow those hackneyed words didn't say what I wanted, but I have enough trouble expressing myself in English.

She smiled and nodded. '*Bu ma fan, bu ma fan. Shan Da, xiao xin.*' No trouble. Be careful, Shan Da. With that, she pressed a crumpled ball of paper into my hand.

It was money, rumpled, dirty bills.

I shook my head and tried to give it back to her but she wouldn't take it. I thanked her again and put it into my jacket pocket.

'*Zai jian*,' she said softly. Goodbye.

I felt my throat thicken as I said, '*Nai-nai, zai jian.*' I went out into the courtyard.

Nai-nai and Xin-hua talked for a minute, then Xin-hua came outside. The two guys were pushing the *che* through the door in the wall into the alley. At the gate I turned and saw Nai-nai standing in the doorway of her house. I waved. She waved. I turned away.

Once in the alley I took off my pack and tossed it onto the flat-bed of the *che*. Then my cane. The camera was already in place inside the washing machine box and the box was tied down securely with thick hemp ropes. I lifted myself onto the *che*, dangling my legs while the committee had a last minute meeting.

Xiao Yang stepped closer, shook hands with me, and said something quickly.

'He says goodbye,' Xin-hua translated, 'and hope you can come back to China someday when the bitter wind no longer is blowing.'

'Goodbye, Xiao Yang,' I said to him, 'and thank you for your help. The three of you saved my life.'

He laughed and shook his head. Xiao Nie said, 'Shan Da, pay close attention to your leg. If bleeding, put the bandage more tight. You have the pills?'

'Yeah.' I patted my breast pocket.

'Wish you safe journey, Shan Da. Hope you can come back someday.'

'I do too,' I said, my voice thick. And as crazy as it sounds, I was telling the truth.

Xin-hua climbed onto the seat and started pedalling. Soon Xiao Nie and Xiao Yang were lost from sight as the *che* rounded a curve in the *hu tong*.

The *che* must have been geared low – probably because sometimes they carried a lot of weight – because Xin-hua's legs were going up and down pretty fast even though we moved at an easy pace. The bumps and shakes immediately started shooting arrows into my leg. I shifted my position a dozen times, finally sitting right up on the *che* behind Xin-hua with my legs stretched out in front of me and crossed, with the wounded one on top. That way my other leg could absorb some of the shocks.

We ambled through a maze of *hu tongs*, most of them busy with mothers with little kids, people going to and from shopping, groups of men and women standing at the little free markets at the intersections, talking. The neighbourhoods looked normal, but I figured I could guess what they were talking about. Once, a news spreader raced past us, his loud-hailer bouncing against his back as he cycled. There were a lot of elementary-age kids playing too, which meant some schools must be closed.

A couple of times, as we crossed over wider *hu tongs*, we saw tanks and trucks lined up, pointing north, ready to roll to Chang An Avenue. Lots of soldiers were there, too, sitting around, playing cards, eating. We crossed those roads as fast as Xin-hua could pedal.

After half an hour of twisting and turning along the *hu tongs,* Xin-hua pulled up under a tree. Her forehead was damp with sweat. She took a swig from the water bottle.

'Shan Da, we are coming to dangerous place.' She pointed ahead. 'Soon this alley will turn to north and go past the Central China Music Academy. After that, it meets Fu Xing Men Avenue. You know that street?'

'Yes.' Fu Xing Men Avenue is the name Chang An Avenue takes once you pass Xi Dan Street going west. Fu Xing Men is the street the Min Zu Hotel and the Yan Jing Hotel are on, the places where the American reporter was transmitting over the two-way. It was the route the PLA had used for the main assault on the square.

'Can't we go another way? There's bound to be millions of PLA around there.'

Right after I said that I felt stupid. After all, we *wanted* to get the PLA on video. Before I could correct the impression I had given her, she explained.

'We have to cross Fu Xing Men somewhere. This way we can cross it and get across Second Ring Road almost at same time.'

I knew what she meant. The Second Ring Road and Fu Xing Men intersected within a half mile of where we were. The Second Ring Road, which follows the line of the old torn-down city wall, is the road the Twenty-seventh Army seemed to be defending against attack from outside the city. They were deployed at major intersections.

'Okay,' I said, 'let's do it.' I pulled off the top of the box, reached down inside, and turned on the camera. Carefully, I fitted the top back on.

'Remember these things, Shan Da. Before we get to Fu Xing Men, you should lying down, pretend to sleep. Don't talk, even if we are stopped.'

Xin-hua turned back around and began to pedal. Soon the *hu tong* widened, then curved to the right. After the curve, on the left, was the gate for the Central China Music Academy. As we passed the gate I saw a soldier scraping a big character poster off the wall beside the gates. The gates were open, but I didn't see any students.

The *hu tong* straightened out and far ahead was the intersection with Fu Xing Men Avenue. On the left was a line of six tanks. On the right, three armoured personnel carriers. The centre of the road was clear and bike traffic moved past the military vehicles.

'Lie down now, Shan Da.'

I stretched out along the *che*'s bed, pretending to sleep, but with my face to the street and my eyes wide open behind the mirror sunglasses that Xiao Yang had given me. The *che* slowed. I could hear Xin-hua's breathing as she pedalled.

A moment later the tracks of a tank loomed up beside me, then the torso of a soldier with an AK 47 slung across his chest. I was so close I could make out the buckle on the Sam Browne belt around his waist and the action of the AK 47. His eyes followed us as we passed him. As he slipped out of view the turret of the tank appeared over his shoulder. The hatch on the tank turret was open and the big machine gun beside it was wrapped in canvas. The turret had a large red star on it.

We got past the tanks without a problem. They didn't look very exciting close up – not like the plastic model American tank on my dresser. These were dark ugly wicked machines, with huge bogey wheels inside wide tracks that would chew a pavement to bits when the tank turned or crush a bicycle like a stick.

We moved out onto Fu Xing Men Avenue westbound bike lane. I continued to lie as if asleep, my head on my arm, as we zig-zagged along.

I wasn't ready for what I saw. The pavement was littered with rocks and bricks, broken glass, even brass shell casings – that must be why Xin-hua was zigzagging around. To avoid all the debris. In places the road surface was ripped up. That would be the tanks. In other places there were burn spots. That would be from molotov cocktails. We passed a solitary shoe. A hat. A smashed pair of glasses. The cement and pipe standards that separated the bike lanes from the main avenue were scattered all over the place, sometimes in piles to form barricades, sometimes mangled and smashed where tanks or armoured personnel carriers had run them over. The avenue looked like a war zone.

We passed a city bus, burned, lying on its side like a dead insect. Then a convoy of crippled troop trucks, tires flat, doors hanging on their hinges, windshields smashed – truck after burned-out truck, still smoking.

All this within about four hundred metres.

'Shan Da! Roadblock ahead. Tanks on bridge. Lots of PLA. Don't moving!'

I sucked in a big breath and let it out slowly. We must be drawing near to the intersection with the Ring Road, I thought. Actually, it wasn't an intersection. It was a bridge, with the Ring Road passing underneath. I began to rehearse what I would say if forced to. Or should I pretend to be dumb? Xin-hua had said not to talk, and she was right. Even if I *could* think up some Chinese to say to a soldier at the roadblock – and I hadn't thought of anything yet – my accent would give me away. I remembered Teacher Huang criticizing me for being sloppy with my tones. I decided to act as if I couldn't speak.

The *che* slowed. I saw troop trucks – at least ten of them – lined up across the roadway so that nothing could pass them going east.

'Soldiers, Shan Da!' Xin-hua hissed.

The *che* stopped. I kept pretending sleep, unmoving, heart pounding. Over by the trucks a soldier walked past, holding a mess tin. A man spoke rapidly, and harshly. Xin-hua answered. She sounded as if she was begging for something.

Silence for a moment. The male voice asked a question, not so nasty this time. I could tell it was a question from the *ma* at the end. Xin-hua laughed – a forced laugh, like a bad actor might give out. She talked some more. The man laughed.

'*Hao!*' said the soldier, and the *che* began to move away. Xin-hua swung to the right in a gradual curve. As we turned I got a good view of the roadblock. Two PLA stood at the end of the bridge with AK 47s in their hands. Beyond them, on the bridge, I counted six tanks, deployed to fend off attack from the west or from the Ring Road below on either side. These guys weren't kidding around.

The *che* picked up speed, bumping down the wide ramp to the Second Ring Road. Xin-hua took us north for fifty yards or so to an intersection then did a U-turn – which was easy because there was no traffic on the road except for a few bikes – and headed south. I lifted my head and looked ahead. When we got back to the bridge she went under and used the momentum from our descent, swinging onto the ramp and pedalling furiously to get up it. Two-thirds of the way up she was puffing like mad and the *che* almost stopped. She jumped off, grabbed the *che*, one hand on the bars, one behind the seat, and heaved, trotting alongside. I've never felt so useless in my life, watching that small woman shove the heavy vehicle up the curved ramp. I knew it would be pointless for me to try to help.

When we got back on Fu Xing Men, Xin-hua jumped on again and pumped the pedals. Her breath rasped in and out. I knew she didn't want to stop for fear of attracting too much attention. We were still very close to the tanks.

We crossed the avenue and turned west again. The avenue on this side of the bridge was only a little less like a war zone. To my relief, the *che* turned right onto a tree-lined street – a bumpy street. It was strange. Suddenly the world looked normal again. A few people walked along the sidewalk. More bikes appeared. Now that we were past the roadblock and I was feeling only scared instead of terrified, my leg began to remind me that there was a groove torn out of my calf. I sat back up again. We passed an intersection with a *hu tong* and I saw a road sign. We were on Zhan Lan Lu. Exhibition Street.

We turned into a little alley and stopped.

Xin Hua's chest was still heaving and the back of her coat was wet through. I was soaked too, but not from working.

'Let's take a short rest,' she puffed. I handed her the water bottle.

'I think I'll turn off the camera, now.'

She nodded, gulping down the water.

I inched myself to the edge of the *che* and let my legs dangle over the side, facing the street. To my left, I could see Fu Xing Men Avenue about a hundred metres away. Across the road was a movie theatre with a big billboard beside it advertising a Gong Fu movie, Bruce Lee style. There were three guys pictured, with fierce faces and sparkling teeth as they sneered, one of them in mid-flight of a flying kick. To the side stood a beautiful woman wearing a long dress with a slit up the leg. She looked scared and helpless and excited, all at the same time.

I looked from her to Xin-hua, squatting on the sidewalk, her breathing regular now, holding the water bottle. Her cotton shoes were frayed at the soles and she had patches on both knees of her slacks. She looked at me and smiled. I think it was then that I understood her courage and how terrified she was.

Standing, she held out the water bottle. 'Thirsty, Shan Da?'

'Thanks.' I took a pull at the bottle and offered it back to her. She shook her head and began to back the *che* out into the street. I put the bottle into her bag with our food tins.

Xin-hua mounted the *che* and started pedalling. We bumped along, continuing north on Exhibition Street. Above the trees that lined the street the grey sky threatened rain. It was quiet, almost peaceful. Xin-hua puffed rhythmically, the *che* creaked, the long bicycle chain from the pedal sprocket to the rear axle rattled softly. Bikes slipped past us, once in a while another *che*.

Ahead was a wide intersection and we drew to a stop at the lights. This street was called Yue Tan Bei Jie. It was wide, with boulevards separating the bike lanes from the main way. Trees in white blossom and shrubs and banks of flowers decorated the boulevards.

Around us a few cyclists stood like storks resting their weight on one leg. On each of the four corners of the intersection was a pair of soldiers. One pair was questioning a man who looked nervously about him as he held out his ID. Across the street I noticed the snout of a tank's cannon poking from a narrow alley. I quickly lay down.

The light changed and we continued north. Shoe-box high rises lined the road on both sides, rising above the trees. The road narrowed. After fifteen minutes or so we passed through another intersection, and Xin-hua braked to a stop at a small *hu tong*.

'What's up?' I asked.

'I get us a cold *qi shui*,' she said softly. While she stood quietly, watching the intersection, I reached into my coat pocket and took out one of my pain pills and one of my antibiotics. *Qi shui* is pop – 'gas water'.

'Our water is almost gone. First wait to see if any PLA around.'

Across from us there was a small store. Xin-hua decided the place was safe and walked quickly over to it. In a few minutes she returned with two Cokes and a half-dozen plastic bottles of lime green liquid. We poured the coke down quickly, burping like mad, and while Xin-hua took back the empties I put the plastic bottles in with the food.

We got underway again. The road was only two lanes wide now, closely lined with trees that formed a canopy overhead.

'This is the Foreign Affairs College,' Xin-hua whispered over her shoulder as we passed a high wall on our right.

At least a dozen soldiers lounged around the main gate up ahead. Two or three looked alert. The rest were squatting, playing cards or talking.

What happened next went past so fast I'm surprised I can remember the details. We hadn't come abreast of the gate yet. A young guy in a yellow T-shirt with SPORT GAME written on it was cycling towards us. A bulging white plastic bag hung from the handlebars. When he was opposite the gate he yelled to the soldiers and flashed a 'V' sign at them, the sign a lot of students had used at Tian An Men Square. One of the troops shouted back. Just as our *che* drew opposite the soldiers – they were only eight or ten metres from us – one of them brought his AK 47 to his shoulder in a lightning move. The barrel jumped as flame shot out and a fraction of an instant later the wicked *crack-crack-crack-crack* deafened me. I took a look across the road in time to see the man slam to the pavement as his bike skewed to the curb and crashed to the dirt at the edge of the road. Green apples tumbled from the bag and rolled into the street. The man lay on the road like a doll some kid had thrown away, his yellow T-shirt already soaked with blood.

By this time the *che* had passed the gate. I felt it surge as Xin-hua shoved with all her might onto the pedals. I heard one of the soldiers laugh and saw two of the card players rush into the street, gathering up the apples.

Suddenly we veered into a narrow *hu tong*. Xin-hua was still pumping like mad on the pedals. We took a sharp turn that almost rolled me off the *che*. I hung on for dear life as Xin-hua cut right again and rushed across a little intersection without looking.

'Xin-hua! Slow down! There's no one behind us!'

She stopped pedalling and we coasted for a moment. Her back heaved. She lay her head down on the handlebars, not looking where we were going. The front tire hit a piece of brick in the road and the bars twisted, steering the *che* against the curb. We bumped to a stop.

Xin-hua got down and turned to face me. She was crying, saying something over and over again in Chinese, pounding a fist into her palm.

My legs and arms tingled as if I had stuck my finger into a light socket. I knew the feeling – the aftereffect of a sudden adrenaline surge. Then the shaking became more violent. I got down from the *che* and put my arms around Xin-hua. She trembled as she cried, her face pressed to my chest.

A woman frowned as she passed us, shaking her head – public displays of affection between men and women are considered very bad manners in China. But I didn't care what she thought.

As we stood in the street like that, it started to rain.

We continued north as soon as we hit a major road again. The rain wasn't very heavy but a wind had come up and dark ugly clouds were moving in. It wasn't long before we came out onto Xi Zhi Men Street across from the zoo. I pictured the map of the city in my head, and knew that we were still pretty much on the route Xin-hua had planned out. This was almost as far north as she had intended to go.

As we headed east on Xi Zhi Men, the dome of the Exhibition Hall came into view. As soon as it did, the brakes of the *che* squealed and we came to a quick stop. The big parking lot of the Exhibition Hall was packed with tanks, troop trucks, and armoured personnel carriers. PLA milled around the lot. A cold hand wrapped icy fingers around my spine. I guessed the same hand grabbed Xin-hua because she did a U-turn as soon as there was a break in the traffic and pedalled west.

We trundled along past the Capital Gymnasium – the parking lot was deserted and the big iron gates were shut tight – and the bus terminal where hundreds of people waited under coloured umbrellas.

We should have known that the PLA would be massed somewhere near here. The Xi Zhi Men Train Station was nearby, and about half a kilometre from the Exhibition Hall there was a major intersection with the Second Ring Road.

Xin-hua turned north just past the Capitol Gym. I knew this road – Bai Shi Qiao. In fifteen minutes or so we'd reach the Friendship Hotel.

The rain came down heavier and the sky darkened. The *che*'s tires hissed on the pavement. Xin-hua turned onto a dirt road that followed a small creek. Within minutes my leg was all pain from the hip down from the bumping and bashing.

The rain seemed to fall more heavily with every metre of bare ground we covered. I began to wonder if Xin-hua had gone nuts from the strain of the last few hours. Where was she taking us?

She finally brought the *che* to a stop in front of a high wall. You could tell it was old from the big grey bricks and the little roof of glazed green tiles on the wall like you see at the Forbidden City, except there the tiles are orange. The gate was gone – burned away it looked like from the marks on the wall.

Once inside the wall Xin-hua jumped off the *che* and pushed it through the long grass towards a small makeshift brick shelter built near the east wall of the compound. It had a roof of corrugated metal but no door. We hurriedly lifted down the box, collected our packs, and took them all into the shelter. Xin-hua went out again and pushed the *che* out of sight behind the building.

Inside, the only light came from an open window on the front wall beside the door. By 'open' I mean just that – no glass, no frame, just a square hole in the wall. Rain swept in through the window and the roof leaked in one corner, but otherwise the dirt floor seemed dry enough.

Xin-hua leaned against the wall and slid down it until she was sitting. She let out a long, tired sigh, folded her arms across her chest, and drew her knees up. Her hair was plastered to her head and water dripped off the ends of her braids. Her face was drawn.

I sat across from her against the back wall so I could see out the door. The rain drummed on the metal roof. I was wet through and uncomfortable, but not cold.

'What is this place?' I asked.

'Workers who are repairing the temple built this to store things and maybe sleep.'

'No, I mean that strange building outside.' As we ducked into the house I had noticed five tall shapes rising into the gloom of the rain.

'Oh. This place is Wu Ta Si, means . . . mmmm . . . five something temple. How I should say those buildings with many roofs?'

I thought for a second. Maybe she meant pagoda.

'Yes. Five Pagoda Temple. My elder brother worked at the zoo. He was ground cleaner. Sometimes I would go visit him at his work and we came here to eating our lunch. Zoo is across the river over there. That's how I know this place.'

'When was that?'

'Maybe five years ago. My brother works in another unit now.'

'So this place is deserted?'

'Should be workers here, but now most workers are stayin
home. Streets are too dangerous, and some are on the strike.'

'Because of what happened in Tian An Men Square?'

'Yes.'

We were silent for a couple of minutes, as if the name of th
place was sacred.

A gust of wind drove rain into the hut. The drops spattered o
the hard-packed dirt.

'Xin-hua, what *did* happen in the square. I don't understan
what it was about. The PLA didn't have to do what they did. The
didn't have to –'

I couldn't say it.

'When I was a little kid, in elementary school, we were taugh
PLA were the heroes.' Xin-hua spoke almost in a whisper, almo
as if I wasn't there and she was talking to herself. 'Sometimes th
PLA soldier would come to the school and talk to us, tell us ho
PLA liberated China before we were born. Since then they fougl
imperialists in the Korea, fought Russians in the north because (
the border argument, fought Vietnam, who were Russia's frienc
at that time.'

I remembered that Lao Xu had told us the Twenty-sevent
Field Army were Vietnam veterans.

'We called those PLA guys Shu-shu, means "Uncle". My elde
brother, when we were very small, had a PLA uniform he wore a
the time, even to school.'

Xin-hua wasn't exactly answering my question, but I let he
talk without interrupting her. You didn't have to be a genius t
see that something she had believed all her life had blown up i
her face and that she was having a tough time coping with that.

As if she had heard my thought she said, 'I don't know wha
happened, Shan Da. But I think the Party and the governmen
especially those old leaders, lost face when Gorbachev was her
and we students were demonstrating in the square. We mad
them look like they couldn't control the country. We made
big mistake. We wanted them to lose face, so they would pa
attention to us.'

She began to cry. 'We never thought,' she sobbed, 'we never thought they would do that to us!'

Cao chuan jie jian, I thought. 'Straw boat borrow arrows'. The government had used the People's Army against the people.

Xin-hua covered her face with her hands and cried harder. I crawled across the dirt floor and sat beside her. I didn't know what to do, so I put my arm around her.

Her crying, the dreary rain, homesickness – everything started to work on me, and I felt my throat thicken. I choked back a sob and tried to keep control.

Xin-hua raised her face from her hands and looked at me. Drops of water stood out on her straight lashes. 'So many of my friends, my classmates, were shot down,' she whispered, 'even one of my teachers. My friends,' she sobbed again, 'I lost my friends.'

I began to cry. 'Me too,' I said.

We sat like that for a long time.

The drumming of the rain on the roof decreased slowly to a light patter. My arm was beginning to feel numb and when I removed it from Xin-hua's shoulder I was glad to see she had dropped off to sleep. Her arms were crossed on her knees and her forehead rested on her arms. Who knows how much sleep she had managed over the last week?

I crawled back across the floor and retrieved my cane. I pulled myself to my feet and hobbled to the Peony box. I pulled off the lid and lifted out the camcorder. It was dry. I put it back into the wire cradle, squeezed the lid onto the box, and hobbled to the door. Outside, rain drizzled out of a heavy grey sky. It was 5:00 P.M. I went outside and walked through the long sodden grass to the walkway. I took a look out the gate, scanning the dirt road in both directions. To my right, in the distance, light traffic moved along Bai Shi Qiao Road. A solitary man fished at the culvert, his long bamboo pole arched over the water. Outside the gate the water meandered slowly around rocks, through the wide riverbed.

I went back inside the temple grounds, walking up the pathway to the tall platform. There were lines of Buddhas carved into the light orange marble wall. Dozens of them. The five pagodas were clearly visible, now that the rainfall had lessened, one at each corner of the platform, the fifth, taller, in the middle. Bells hung from the ends of some of the eaves. Lao Xu had once told me the bells were to keep evil spirits away.

I walked around the platform. All over, in the long grass, were fallen pillars, rubble, pieces of green tile – not the kind of destruction that the passing of time would cause. Then I remembered that, during the Cultural Revolution that ended about ten years ago, gangs of Red Guards would swarm into temples, museums, and other historical monuments, smashing things up and defacing everything they could reach. Something to do with stopping the worship of old customs.

When I got back to the little house the rain had come on strong again. Xin-hua was still asleep. I lowered myself to the floor again, opposite the door, staring out at the rain beating the grass, listening to the hammering on the roof.

I looked at Xin-hua , hunched over, her head on her slender arms. If I ever got to the embassy, ever got out of this place, I would hate to leave her behind. I don't mean I was falling in love with her, or any of that soap-opera stuff. I was *worried* about her. What would happen when I left? It was easy for me. I could leave this country – at least, I *hoped* I could. But what would happen to her?

I imagined her in Canada, goggle-eyed at all the strange things she'd see. Especially how rich people are. The freedom we have. And then I began to compare her to the kids I knew, the ones my age, the older ones who had gone to university. That gave me a funny feeling. Things at home would seem different now. I knew, I just knew that from now on there would be some kind of gap between me and the other kids. We were all pretty well off, at least the people I hung around with. All the guys could drive. They all lived in nice houses, some with pools in the yard, most with basketball hoops over the garage door. Colour TVs, VCRs, a late-model car in the driveway. And that's what most of the guys wanted when they got through school. A good job, meaning one that paid lots of money. A cottage in Muskoka.

If I told them that in China one of those little washing machines was a status symbol, they'd laugh. If I told them about Nai-nai's house and how peaceful her courtyard was, they'd tell me to get real. But whose world was more real? Ours, or the world Xin-hua lived in?

She was different from the girls I knew, too. Really different. Their idea of a tragedy was running out of mousse or breaking a fingernail. They were a lot like the woman I had seen this morning on the movie billboard. They were almost all heavily into feminism and talked about being taken seriously as *persons* while they put on purple lipstick. I don't know. Maybe I was being too hard on them. But nobody I knew was like Xin-hua. To me, she was a hero. A strong woman with more character than most of the kids I knew, male or female, put together.

Including me.

It was five o'clock and still pouring rain so I lay down on the dirt and tried to get comfortable. I closed my eyes and tried to sleep.

六月

九

日

June 9

It was a long night. The rain came and went. The wind blustered,
hissing in the long grass, moaning around the pagodas. At least
a thousand times I imagined I heard a platoon of PLA come
charging through the gate, equipment rattling, to drag us out of
the brick hut and throw us against the ancient wall of the temple
and shoot us. After the first dozen times I stopped getting up and
checking the gate.

Towards dawn the wind came up stronger and I guess it blew
away the rain, because when I finally decided there was no use
trying to sleep anymore the rain had stopped. I went outside to go

to the bathroom – only there wasn't one, of course. It was still grey outside, but the cloud was higher up and moving at quite a clip. Xin-hua woke up when she heard the lunch tins rattling as I pried off the lids. I was starving and I was pretty sure she was worse off than me.

She smiled at me and rubbed the sleep from her eyes.

'Hungry?' I asked.

She nodded and looked a little embarrassed. 'I back in a minute.'

She went outside. While she was gone I took the top off the washing machine box and set it on the dirt floor as a makeshift table. I put a lunch tin on each side, along with two of the plastic bottles of green stuff. Luckily Nai-nai had put a set of chopsticks in with each lunch.

We attacked the rice and pickled vegetables. The green stuff Xin-hua had bought the day before tasted like sugar with sugar added, but at least it was wet.

My leg seemed better. I could put more weight on it. I hoped it wouldn't flare up too much with the travelling it would get. I had two pain pills left, and I wanted to save them until I needed them.

Xin-hua and I figured that with luck and without any mishaps, we should be able to get to the embassy sometime during the afternoon. The thing was, she emphasized, not to try to move too quickly or else we would attract attention. I knew what she meant. We had to blend in, which was hard enough with my tall lanky build and my sunglasses on a cloudy day. We had to be two workers, delivering a washing machine for a lucky owner, taking it easy along the way.

We set out into the teeth of a stiff wind, bouncing our way back to Bai Shi Qiao Road, the tires of the *che* squishing and slipping in the mud. We turned north. Bikes hissed past, bells jingling, as people went to work. Soon we passed the wide front gate of the Friendship Hotel. When I had been there with Eddie and Dad the place was bustling, with taxis and tour buses and bikes going in and out of the open gates. Now it looked like the place was closed. There was a soldier by the gate house and the wide gates were shut. Xin-hua pedalled more slowly as we passed.

'Seems the foreigners have all left,' she commented.

I didn't say anything. I was thinking. Past the hotel, near the intersection with the Third Ring Road, I called out to Xin-hua.

'Hold up a sec.'

'What?' she said, still pedalling.

'Stop, please.'

Xin-hua steered the *che* off the pavement.

'I have an idea, Xin-hua. I don't know why I didn't think of it before. Why don't we go into the Friendship Hotel! I could use the phone to call the embassy.' It all seemed so easy, I felt like a fool for not thinking of it long before.

Xin-hua shook her head. 'Shan Da, I can't go in there. Chinese not allowed in the hotel without special permission.'

I had forgotten about that. Chinese couldn't get into a hotel where foreigners stayed unless they had business there and the papers to prove it. They couldn't get into the Friendship Store either, unless they had connections.

'Okay, you're right. But how about if you wait outside and I go in?'

She shook her head again. 'Shan Da, you look Chinese now, remember?'

I put my hand up to my hair, still stiff with black polish, and a little dirty from lying on the floor of the hut. 'But I can still speak English to the guard. He'll believe me, don't you think?'

Again the irritating head shake. 'No passport, Shan Da. No ID. You could be anybody. PLA are looking for students who are running away.'

She started to pedal again, sure that my idea was dumb. Which it was, I realized now. Until I got to the embassy, I was nobody. I was a worker delivering a washing machine, whether I liked it or not.

We turned onto the Third Ring Road, a wide avenue that headed east past high rises and stores and lots of construction sites. The crane towers rose silent and unmoving into the dull sky like bits of giant building sets left unfinished by a child.

I was just saying to Xin-hua that on this road at least the pavement was fairly smooth when we spotted them in the distance. A convoy of trucks, packed full with troops, bristling with rifles held upright by the soldiers. Heading towards us. As the convoy advanced the people on the sidewalks scattered, disappearing down side streets and into stores. Cyclists pressed on, looking down at the road as they pumped, or found reasons to swing onto side streets.

Which is exactly what Xin-hua did. She hunched her shoulders, as if remembering the shots that flew over her head yesterday, and made a sharp turn to the right onto a tree-lined street, and increasing her speed.

So we headed back south, the direction from which we had come that morning.

Eventually we turned east, then north, I think, then we zigged and zagged along a narrow alley through a quiet neighbourhood and came out near the Huang Si, the Yellow Temple. My leg had started to stiffen up again, and I kept shifting my weight and changing my position.

Suddenly Xin-hua braked to a stop. She climbed onto the platform with me.

'Shan Da, do you have map? Want to show you something.'

I got out my map and we opened it carefully, looking around, and spread it on the bed of the *che*, hiding it with out bags and legs. We didn't want some Public Security Bureau type or PLA guy to see us poring over a map that was only sold in tourist hotels.

Pointing out various streets as she talked, Xin-hua explained the problem. To get to the San Li Tun embassy compound, which is where the Canadian Embassy was located, we had to either take the Second Ring Road – the road the PLA was defending so aggressively with all the tanks and troops – for a kilometre or two, or we could cross it by going south on He Ping Li Street, turn east on Dong Zhi Men Street, and cross it again. The reason was that outside the Second Ring Road, where we were then, there were no streets through a big area called Zuo Jia Zhuang.

Either route was risky. The Second Ring Road was PLA territory. That's where we had run up against the roadblock yesterday. Inside the Second Ring Road there were PLA all over the place, at all the big intersections. And that's where the plain clothes PLA were operating, not to mention the bands of club-wielding Public Security cops.

I opted for crossing the Ring Road. 'We can blend in better on the side streets,' I said, 'even if there are more PLA around. On the Ring Road we'll be too easy to notice.'

'Yes, I agree.'

'Okay, let's do it,' I said, trying to sound confident. 'And let's turn on the camcorder now.'

Xin-hua swallowed hard and nodded. She remounted and started pedalling. It was 12:15 P.M.

We went south and got across the Ring Road okay. It was a little tense, but the troops at the roadblock, as near as I could tell as I lay there pretending to be asleep, seemed bored by the whole thing. Xin-hua talked to them for only a moment or two and we were on our way again.

There were soldiers at every intersection now. They seemed to be stopping citizens at random, especially ones in their late teens and early twenties, and checking their ID. When we turned east onto Dong Zhi Men, two troops held a young woman at gunpoint, kneeling in the gutter. Her wailing cut the air as the gun barrels jabbed into her back.

When we approached the Ring Road again my heart was pounding. I was sure it could be heard by the PLA at the roadblock, resonating against the boards of the *che*. I counted four voices this time, in addition to Xin-hua's. She was trying to sound friendly, chattering away to them, but her voice was forced.

I was curled up into a ball, pretending to sleep, my canvas bag with the battery packs in it tucked out of sight against my chest. I heard a voice right next to my head. A rough bossy voice. Xin-hua answered. Then something round and hard prodded my back. A machine-gun barrel.

I pretended to wake up, with a wide phony yawn. My pulse banged at my temples. A soldier with a broad flat nose and a thin moustache prodded me again, rattling away in Chinese. I forced a smile and nodded. Then I pointed to my ears and mouth and shook my head.

The soldier motioned with his gun barrel for me to hand over the two canvas bags. I gave him Xin-hua's. He opened it, looked inside, and tossed it back to me, then motioned again. Trembling, I handed him mine.

That morning I had put my battery packs and video cassettes into the lunch tins. The soldier dumped the tins out. They clattered onto the bed of the *che*, but luckily the lids didn't pop open.

'*Chi wan le ma?*' he said, laughing. Have you eaten yet?

'*Chi wan le.*' Xin-hua answered.

The soldier said something else to Xin-hua and she reached into her jacket pocket and handed over her green *hu kou* card. She hadn't brought her university ID because the PLA were arresting students left and right.

The soldier tossed it back at her. It hit her in the chest and then fell to the pavement. She dismounted and picked it up, put it away, and stood there.

The soldier growled something to me.

'*Ta mei you.*' Xin-hua said nervously. He doesn't have it. Then she talked some more. I guessed she was giving him some phony story to explain why I didn't have my ID. She reached into her pants pocket and drew out some crumpled bills and as she talked she moved her hands around so that the money was visible. I got the idea and pulled out the wad of one and two yuan notes that Nai-nai had given me. The soldier accepted both gifts. He seemed satisfied. While he and Xin-hua talked, another soldier, a squat, thick-set character who obviously enjoyed carrying an AK 47 around, pointed to the washing machine box.

My heart hammered at my ribs. I swallowed with a dry throat.

Xin-hua started chattering away like crazy. I could already picture us kneeling in the street with the AK 47s jabbing the backs of our necks.

The heavy-set guy barked an order. Xin-hua argued. He

shouted at her. She climbed up on the *che* and stood beside the box.

As she bent to grasp the lid she whispered, 'When I shout, run Shan Da!'

I was paralyzed. My limbs shook. Run? How far would I get? *She* was the one who should run, but how could I argue with her in English?

She paused, looked at both soldiers, and forced a laugh that didn't convince anybody. Then she grasped the lid firmly.

Crack-crack-crack!

I swear her mouth was opening to shout whatever it was that she thought would divert the soldiers' attention when gunfire blasted behind us, out on the Ring Road. The soldiers turned towards the gunfire. Xin-hua looked at me, her eyes wide with terror. Then the soldiers took off, running towards the tanks that lined the road.

In a split second Xin-hua was back on the seat, pedalling like mad. We kept our heads down as we crossed the Ring Road. Off to our left in the distance, two men were running along the road. Gunfire sounded again and one of them collapsed to the ground. The second figure stopped dead in his tracks and raised his hands. Just as we crossed the roadway they shot him where he stood.

I covered my eyes with my trembling hands, screaming inside my skull.

Soon we reached a really busy area and realized we were in big trouble. The whole place was thick with green uniforms. The quiet, tree-lined streets leading off Dong Zhi Men to our right led into the San Li Tun embassy area, and every street was guarded by a contingent of PLA who were stopping vehicles and pedestrians who tried to get in. Xin-hua kept right on going past San Li Tun, the street we wanted. We came to an intersection at a wide avenue and I realized we had reached the Third Ring Road. She pulled to the curb and stopped.

'I go back, see what's going on,' she said.

'Okay.' I hardly noticed her words. I was still trying to control my nerves after the adrenaline rush caused by our narrow escape.

And by the sight of the man with his hands up getting shot in the back.

I looked around. The street wasn't very busy. The odd bus went by. There was a big park-like place across the Ring road from me and beyond the wide iron fence I saw the outlines of tents pitched on the grounds. The friendly PLA, I thought, doing a boy scout operation on the grounds of the Beijing Agricultural Exhibition Centre. Up the road to the north a tall silver-gray monstrosity rose above the trees into the grey sky – the Great Wall Hotel. Below, a solitary taxi crawled out onto the road and came towards me.

As it passed, I got an idea. Why not just hail a taxi?

But I guess the adrenaline rush had affected my brain. I forgot, as I had outside the Friendship Guest House, that I was in disguise. And suddenly it hit me with the force of a train at high speed that the disguise was now a trap. I was imprisoned by it, stuck.

There I was, between an embassy I couldn't even get to because I looked Chinese and a hotel I couldn't enter for the same reason.

I looked up and saw Xin-hua coming towards me, walking quickly.

'I waited across street from a roadblock until I saw a woman PLA turned away,' she panted. 'Then I follow her and ask to talk this thing with her. She said PLA are stopping everyone who tries get into the area because too many Chinese trying to get out of China. They are apply for visa. Biggest tries are Canada and U.S. Even if you have Chinese passport, PLA make you reapply now for another one. That takes weeks.'

I knew that in China the average citizen couldn't get a passport. They had to have permission from the state and from their work unit. People who got them were lucky – usually students going abroad or people on business, or if they had relatives abroad.

'Government is very angry,' Xin-hua went on. 'A famous Chinese scientist, Fang Li-zhi, and his wife are hiding in American Embassy. So that's why so many PLA here.'

Xin-hua looked pretty dejected. 'I'll take us around block, Shan Da, but I don't think we can get to your embassy. I'm sorry. I should have thought of that.'

She wasn't half as sorry as I was. Now what? I thought. But I didn't say that to her.

'Come on, Xin-hua, it's not your fault. How could you know this would happen?'

Xin-hua slapped the curb angrily as she spoke. 'But now what to do? My friends and I didn't think this enough. Now you look too Chinese. If not, you could walk past those PLA and be safe.' She slapped the curb again, so hard it must have hurt her. 'We should have brought your clothes. And soap to clean your hair.'

We sat there, silent, for a while. I got up and took the box top off. I shut off the camera, removed the cassette and battery pack and exchanged them for new ones, and put the exposed cassette into one of the food tins. I tossed the battery into the gutter. I fixed the top back onto the box.

I sat down again, closer to Xin-hua. 'Don't worry,' I said. 'I've been thinking. We're right close to the road to the airport, right? I think I might as well go there. The foreigners all have to go to the airport to get out anyway. Maybe Dad is already there. And look, Xin-hua, we got everything on video. Those jerks at the roadblock, the microphone will have picked them up. And the PLA blocking the embassy area. We got that, too. Everything we've seen, all that horrible stuff, is going to make it to the outside. The government won't be able to say it didn't happen. We've got the proof. And that's what we – you and your friends and I – what we wanted.'

Xin-hua wiped the water from her eyes. 'Yes,' she said. The determination was back in those dark eyes of hers. 'I go back to store over there and buy something to drink.'

'But we gave all our money to that soldier at the roadblock.'

She smiled. 'I kept one yuan back. I knew we would be thirst soon.'

By mid-afternoon the cloud cover was breaking up and the sun was trying to push through but not quite making it. We trundled north on the Third Ring Road to where it intersected with the airport road and then turned right onto the airport road. The two-lane, tree-lined road stretched straight as an arrow into the distance. I remembered coming the opposite way, what seemed so long ago, at night, full of anticipation and a great sense of adventure. Well, no way could I say I hadn't had adventure.

I was pretty jumpy. Xin-hua and I talked as she puffed along, her body swaying from left to right as she pedalled. We were pretty sure there'd be more roadblocks along here somewhere. Xin-hua figured there'd be one between the big foreign hotel compound and the airport. I wanted to get off the *che* and walk the rest of the way once we saw the first roadblock, but so far she hadn't agreed. I argued with her. At least I had a chance to get through. I could convince them I was Canadian, take off my coat and shirt if I had to and show them my fish-belly white skin and my baby blues. But she had no alibi. The washing machine gambit got less credible the closer we got to the airport. She said she could say she lived on one of the farms nearby. The land around us was all under cultivation and we could see buildings in the distance through the trees. I didn't buy that. She didn't look like a brigade member, not with her light skin and soft student's hands.

As we talked and argued and planned, taxis sped past us, full of worried-looking foreigners. The occasional tour bus full of disappointed tourists rumbled by us, too. Wonder what you said on your postcards home, I thought. *Dear Fred, glad you're not here. Be home earlier than expected, if I don't get killed. Love, Ethel.*

Every once in a while a troop truck roared by. They went in both directions. Which didn't seem too efficient to me. Every time a truck full of green uniformed men appeared Xin-hua's shoulders would tense up and she'd pedal harder and I'd feel my nerve ends screaming at me.

We crossed a bridge over a wide river and just after we crossed over, Xin-hua turned the *che* off the road and we bumped along a dirt track. In a moment we were out of sight behind the trees. She got down and said, 'Let's take a short rest, Shan Da.'

It was pretty warm by then in spite of the steady breeze. The sun was gradually burning off the rest of the clouds. We took off our jackets and caps and followed a path through the trees down to the river. I had to step carefully to get down the steep path. Along the edge of the wide, slow-moving brown water the long grass, tops bent by the breeze, hid us from view.

Xin-hua sat down on the bank and rolled up her pant legs to the knees, then the sleeves of her shirt. She waded into the water, splashing it onto her face and arms. I wished I could do the same. After all, I hadn't washed in two days. But the water wasn't exactly sparkling clear, and I was afraid of infection.

But I did take off my shoes and socks and stand in the warm water up to my ankles. The dark mud squirmed between my toes as I splashed water on my face and arms. Then I had an idea. I ran my wet hands through my hair and looked at them. Very little of the shoe polish came off on my hands. So much for that idea.

We sat down on the bank, each of us propped against a poplar so that we faced each other, our outstretched legs almost touching. Xin-hua leaned her head back against the smooth bark and closed her eyes.

You'd never have known that we were on the edge of a city of almost eight million people. Sunlight flooded from behind a cloud onto the river. The water murmured through the tall reeds and in the trees birds sang to one another. I closed my eyes.

It would have been a nice peaceful rest, but my mind was buzzing like a transformer on overtime. Would I get to the airport? Would Dad be there? What would happen to Xin-hua *then*?

The distant rumble of a jet taking off startled me. A troop truck roared across the bridge.

What should I do? I opened my eyes and looked at Xin-hua. I knew that if I asked her, she would take me all the way to the airport – if we could get past the PLA, which we couldn't. The lower the danger level for me, the higher for her. She had been responsible for me since Tian An Men Square. At least, I knew that she felt responsible. Now I felt responsible for her.

What I wanted to do was separate from her right there. She had come far enough. I could take my camcorder and the unused batteries and throw them into the river, dump the box, and send her back home on the *che*. She'd be safe on her own as long as she was careful.

I got up quietly and limped up to the *che*. I took the last two bottles of green pop down to the riverbank and laid one in Xin-hua's lap. Her eyes opened.

'Thank you, Shan Da.'

She closed her eyes again. I chewed my pop open and sucked the sticky sweet stuff out of the container. It didn't quench my thirst at all.

Xin-hua sat up and rubbed her eyes. She bit a hole into the top of her pop and started to drink it.

'You must be tired,' I said.

'What time is it?'

'Four o'clock.'

'We should go,' she said, tossing the plastic container into the river.

'Um, I've been thinking of that, Xin-hua. I think I can go on my own from here. I can walk. And maybe I can hitch a ride from a taxi or a tour bus.'

I didn't really believe that, and I guess she didn't either. She shook her head without even thinking about what I had said.

'No, no. We go together.'

I tried to explain my thinking to her, but she wouldn't listen. The only part she agreed with was that we probably wouldn't need the camcorder anymore, and therefore the battery packs, and she shouldn't have them on her, so we should do as I said and throw them in the river. But that was it.

'You can't go alone,' she insisted. 'When PLA stop you, you can't speak Chinese and they can't speak English. You need me interpret for you if trouble.'

So I tried to make a deal with her. 'Okay, I'll let you stay with me till we get to the foreign hotel compound.'

'No, still too far from airport. I stay with you until Airport Guest House. Then I back to my house.'

We talked some more, but trying to get her to change her mind was like taking the Great Wall apart brick by brick. So we tossed the camcorder and the battery packs out into the river. After a few moments' thought I threw the audio cassettes into the river too. I knew there was no way I'd forget what was recorded on them. I put the video cassettes and the two rolls of film into my pants pockets. Then we untied the box, tipped it off the *che*, and stamped it flat. We pushed the *che* out onto the road and away we went.

The tall poplars along the road cast long shadows ahead of us. Xin-hua had left her coat on the back of the *che* but she kept her cap on against the sun. I had to keep on my coat so my white arms wouldn't show. The breeze at our backs had picked up and seemed to push us towards the roadblock we knew would be waiting.

Two troop trucks were parked at the gate to the foreign hotel compound and four PLA stood outside the gate house. We got past without being challenged. There was some local traffic on the road here – a few bikes, a couple of donkey carts. They must have been from the farms, coming back empty from the free markets in the city.

We saw the roadblock long before we arrived at it. It was set up at a 'Y' in the road. The road to the airport curved to the left and just past the 'Y' there were enough PLA to storm a small village. Two troop trucks blocked the road, leaving enough room between them for one vehicle to squeeze through.

As we approached, three shots rang out.

Xin-hua flinched. I felt that cold hand of dread again pinching my spine and squeezing my chest. I could hardly breathe. The thudding of my heart resonated in my skull.

'Xin-hua! Stop and turn around!'

She kept pedalling, head down. 'Remember, Shan Da. Don't talk.'

I reached into my pockets and took out the 8mm cassettes. I opened my pants and jammed the cassettes down the front, inside my underwear. The rolls of film I tucked into my shirt pocket. I buttoned my coat to the neck.

There was no use lying down and doing my sleepy worker impersonation. Nobody would believe I could sleep through the sound of gunfire. So I sat with my legs dangling over the side of the *che*. I wanted to be able to get down fast if I needed to.

A taxi passed us just as we drew near, so we waited behind it while the soldiers checked it out. The four passengers and driver handed over their papers. There were a dozen or so troops sitting smoking and talking on either side of the road. Two lean, hard-looking guys were doing the checking. On the right side of the road an armoured personnel carrier was parked in the trees. The hatch was open and a soldier manned the machine gun on top.

Off in the trees to the left I could see a couple of tents. Next to one of the tents three men in civilian clothes lay on the ground. I couldn't see them very well through the trees, but I could tell they wore light shirts and dark pants.

And I knew by the way they lay, arms and legs tangled, that they were dead.

'Xin-hua!' I hissed, 'we've got to –'

Just then the taxi was waved through the slot between the front bumpers of the trucks. One of the guards barked at Xin-hua. She pedalled up closer and stopped when the second soldier held his hand up.

The two guys here weren't like the men we had seen in the city. Both were wiry, with cold eyes and straight faces. They had their AK 47s slung on their backs and, in spite of the heat, they had their helmets and coats on. They had four pockets on their coats. They were officers.

The first one snapped a question at Xin-hua. She answered him, probably spinning out the story she had dreamed up, that we were from one of the nearby brigades and were on our way to the Airport Guest House to see if we could drum up a little hauling business with the *che*. She forced a little laugh but the soldier's face was like a slab of stone.

He said something else and she talked some more. She was going on and on about something that I couldn't follow at all. But I could see the soldier was getting impatient. He turned to the troops sitting at the side of the road and snapped out an order. Three of them jumped up, threw down their cigarettes and ran over to the *che*.

I could hear the panic creeping into Xin-hua's voice as she started explaining again. Two of the troops stepped forward and hauled her bodily from the *che*, gripping her arms. The third started going through her pockets. One of them said something and the other two laughed. I hopped off the *che*, wincing when I landed on my right leg. I had taken only one step towards Xin-hua before the second officer swung his machine gun from behind his back in a lightning move and jabbed the barrel into my stomach. I gasped, unable to move. The pain was incredible.

One of the soldiers yanked the green ID from Xin-hua's pocket and spoke to the officer. I heard her name in the rush of words.

The officer clipped out another order and the soldier with the gun barrel in my stomach lifted it, pushing off my glasses. He uttered an exclamation of surprise when he saw my eyes, then brought the gun barrel higher to flick my cap off my head. He said something to me.

Xin-hua spoke up. I heard *bu hui*, not able. She was telling them I was deaf and dumb. The officer in front of me just laughed. Lowering his gun he reached out one hand and yanked at the front of my jacket. Two buttons popped off and fell onto the road. Then he ripped my shirt open.

'*Ta shi wai guo ren!*' he crowed. He's a foreigner!

I knew we were sunk now. And I knew Xin-hua was in deep trouble. I looked over at her. The two troops still held her with her arms pinned to her sides. Her eyes were wide with panic and she breathed in short, quick gasps.

A storm of talk followed. The two officers and Xin-hua all spoke at once. I heard the word *foreigner* a few times and Xin-hua said *Jia na da ren* several times. She was telling them I was a Canadian, so I figured she was trying to cover for me. The talk stopped for a second.

'*Ni shi xue sheng, dui bu dui?*' The officer interrogating her asked. You're a student aren't you?

'*Bu. Gong ren.*' No. A worker.

Her head snapped back when he slapped her. If the two soldiers hadn't been holding her the force of the blow would have knocked her down.

'Wait! Leave her alone! She isn't –'

The officer drove his gun barrel into my stomach again and I dropped to my knees, gasping, hands to my stomach.

The officer with Xin-hua barked an order and the two troops began to lead her off towards the trees.

'Shan Da, don't fight them! Do as they say!' she yelled over her shoulder. One of the soldiers slugged her on the side of the head and she fell to her knees. The other kicked her in the back. Then they hauled her to her feet and dragged her into the trees.

I turned to the officer who had been talking to her. 'Please, she has nothing to do with this! Please don't hurt her!'

He pointed between the troop trucks, towards the airport, with his gun barrel. 'You go.' He shouted. 'Now!'

I took a limping step towards him. 'Please,' I pleaded, 'please don't hurt her. Let her go. Please!'

'Go! *Kuai!*' Quickly!

I tried to calm my voice. Maybe I could get to him if I could sound more reasonable. 'Look, is there anybody here who speaks English?' I asked.

I heard a car pull up behind me as I tried again. 'Please let me talk to your commanding officer. I just want to –'

Crack!

The sound of a single gunshot. I turned to look into the trees where they had taken Xin-hua.

'Oh god, no,' I moaned. 'No, no, noooooo!' I heard my own voice rise to a scream. I flew at the officer, fingers tearing at his face. 'You bastard! You bastard! You bloody bastard!'

Iron hands clutched me from behind and tore me away from him. He swung the AK 47 around and up, catching me sharply under the chin, sending a shock wave of pain along my jaw and knocking me backwards into the man behind me. He pulled back the action of the machine gun. A rapid-fire flow of words burst from behind my head. The man in front lowered his weapon, scowling, turned and shouted to the troops from the side of the road who had moved towards us. Three of them grabbed me roughly, one on each arm and one behind. The one behind grabbed a handful of my hair and yanked back.

The troops dragged me bodily away. There was a lot of furious yelling. A car door opened. The three troops manhandled me to the taxi that stood there, engine running. There were two men in the front seat staring straight ahead. The back door was open. The soldiers bent me over and shoved me into the cab so hard I smashed my head on the window crank of the opposite door. Someone bent my legs towards the small of my back, sending a searing spear of pain into my right calf. The car door slammed and the taxi roared away.

The taxi careened along the road for about five minutes, then swung up the long curved ramp to the airport terminal and screeched to a stop. Both men jumped out of the cab. I lay there, dazed, trying to shake some sense into my head. The door at my feet opened and the taxi driver tapped my leg, saying something. I struggled slowly into a sitting position. I winced when he took my legs and swung them out the cab door. Once my feet were out and on the pavement, it was easy for him to reach in and help me out of the car and onto my feet.

I stood swaying a little and turned to see the other passenger rushing through the glass doors with a big suitcase in his hand. I think I said thank you to the cab driver, then limped towards the door myself. Once inside, I felt like I was swimming in a soup of noise and confusion. I just couldn't take it, couldn't get my bearings. People rushed past, some pulling suitcases on wheels, this way and that. Voices in three or four languages blasted over a loudspeaker.

I took a few steps and stopped again.

I'm not sure how long I stood there in the chaos but I slowly came to my senses. Sort of. I looked around at the crazy house of the airport. There were ticket check-ins straight across from me. The milling crowd collected in thick clots at each wicket, pushing and pressing, waving tickets and shouting. I limped to a counter with a sign above it: INFORMATION.

The man behind the counter exclaimed something in Chinese when he saw me and pulled a clean handkerchief out of his pocket. He handed it to me. I wiped the blood from my face as best I could.

Without waiting for me to speak, he asked, 'What country you from?'

'Canada.'

'Canada upstairs.' He indicated a wide stairway at the far end of the hall. 'This all United States down here.'

Silently I turned and hobbled to the stairs. People rushed by, not seeming to take any notice of me. I got to the stairway and was relieved to see an escalator there. But it wasn't running. Gripping the handrail with both hands, I pulled my way up the wide staircase.

At the top, I stopped. I felt dizzy and held onto the bannister for a moment. When the woozy feeling passed I wiped my face again. The cut on my forehead was still bleeding. I walked along a wide hallway. People sat along the walls, talking quietly, suitcases and backpacks lined up in front of them. I came to a wide lounge full of people. One wall of the lounge was a big picture window. A counter stretched along the far wall. People stood before it in quiet lines. A sign on the wall said Information Registration.

I limped towards the sign, drawing stares from the tired, scared-looking people around me. A woman in front of me turned away from the counter, almost bumping into me.

'My god!' she said. 'Excuse me. I'm sorry.' She hurried away, passport in hand.

The woman behind the counter had a big loose leaf binder open in front of her with dog-eared sheets of paper filled with names. Her eyebrows jumped and her mouth dropped open when she looked up and saw me. But her voice was cool and professional.

'Do you need medical aid?'

'Is my father here? I have to find my father. Or Eddie. Maybe Eddie is here. Lao Xu isn't here because he's dead. They killed him.'

'What's your name, son?'

'They killed Xin-hua, too. They tried to kill me, but Xin-hua made them leave me alone. She saved me. She got me out.'

'Son, listen. What's your name? You tell me your name, okay? Are you Canadian?'

'Shan Da.'

'What?'

'It means big mountain,' I explained. 'Because I'm tall.'

'Son, what's your name. What's your father's name?'

'Um, Ted. Ted Jackson.'

She ran her finger down the lists, up and down, up and down. 'Edward Jackson? Canadian? From Toronto?'

'He's a news cameraman.'

'He's here, son. At least, he registered here . . . let me see . . . yesterday.'

I turned away from the counter and walked slowly back down the centre aisle examining all the people in the chairs and on the floor on my right. When I reached the end of the aisle I turned and started back, this time scanning the chairs on the window side.

My father was sitting in the last seat in one of the rows, closest to the window.

His long legs stretched out into the space between the seats. His jeans were rumpled and creased. He wore a white T-shirt. He hadn't shaved in days and his long, light brown hair was greasy and uncombed.

He moved. He drew his legs towards him and leaned his fore-arms on his thighs. He stared at the floor between his feet.

I limped towards the window and stopped in front of him. He didn't raise his head at first. The people on either side of him murmured to one another, sneaking glances at me.

After a few moments my father looked up and the flat light from the window fell across his pale, haggard features. His blue eyes seemed dull and without energy. I realized he didn't recognize me as I stood before him in torn, dirty Chinese clothes, face bloody, cap pulled down over my dyed hair. He looked down at his feet again.

Then he looked up again. He searched my face, his eyes coming alive.

My father rose slowly to his feet, saying nothing, keeping his eyes fixed on my face. When he had reached his full height his mouth began to quiver and tears streamed from his eyes. He stepped towards me and put his arms around me and his body shook with deep sobs.

I stood with my arms hanging at my sides. 'Dad,' I said, 'they killed her. They killed Xin-hua. They killed Lao Xu. They killed everybody.'

June 28

Dad told me afterwards that we got a plane out early the next morning. The airport was a total crazy house. A lot of the people who boarded the plane that the Canadian government had chartered to take us out had no baggage, and some, like me, had no ID or passport. We all got past the airport security anyway. People from the embassy shepherded everybody along. The only people the security guards – they were regular airport security, not PLA – the only people they stopped to question were those who looked Chinese.

I don't remember anything about the flight home. I was

sedated the whole way. So this time I was the one who was 'blasted.'

We flew directly to Vancouver, then through to Toronto. The entire trip took about twenty hours. I slept through almost the whole thing, even in the transit lounge at Vancouver Airport. Mom met us at Toronto and drove us home in the dark.

By the time she pulled her Audi into our driveway the sedatives had mostly worn off. My body still felt tired and heavy and my mind was a bit numb, like I wasn't too interested in what was going on around me. I was just sort of passive. That's the only way I can describe it.

Mom and Dad clucked and fussed around me. First thing they did was order me upstairs to have a bath. I guess I smelled pretty bad. My Chinese clothes were dirty and bloody, with a couple of days' sweat soaked into them.

The bathroom was clean and dry, the overhead light shining on the blue and white tiles, and the air smelled of soap and shaving lotion. Dad was standing beside me dumping bubble bath into the water, telling me I'd probably have to get a really short haircut because the shoe polish wasn't going to come out very easily. I unzipped my pants and let them fall to my ankles, then pushed down my underwear.

Four 8mm video cassettes clattered to the tile floor.

'What the –' Dad exclaimed. 'Alex! Are those what I think they are?'

The sight of the cassettes and the noise they made when they hit the floor snapped me back to reality. 'There's two rolls of film in my shirt pocket,' I said. 'I put them there when –'

Dad gathered up the tapes, retrieved the film, and put them on the sink, then helped me into the bath. I lowered myself down into the hot, soapy water.

Mom came into the bathroom. She put the lid of the toilet seat down and sat there chain-smoking while I talked. She was well-dressed, as usual, and had a new hairdo. Her hands shook as she lit her cigarettes.

Dad sat on the floor, leaning against the cabinet, shuffling the tapes like thick black cards. He looked whacked, and he needed a bath as much as I did. And a shave.

A few minutes later I was giving Mom and Dad a condensed account of what had happened to me since the night of the fourth. Dad knew Lao Xu and Xin-hua were dead because I had told him at the airport. But when I got to the part where Xin-hua was murdered, Mom started crying. Her carefully made-up face twisted in anger and she kept saying, 'How could they? How could they?'

Dad stopped fiddling with the tapes and stared down at them. I knew what he was thinking. He looked up at me, at my eyes. I knew he understood that we owed it to Xin-hua to get the contents of the tapes and films on the news.

Then it was Dad's turn. He told me that on the night of the fourth, he was shooting tape fast and furious on Chang An Avenue – the burning armoured personnel carrier, the students helping the soldiers out, the soldiers disappearing into the crowd, all of it made a perfect image. Then the troop trucks came and the soldiers jumped down from the trucks and started to fan out. He saw a knot of uniformed men coming at him in his viewfinder.

'I tried to outrun them – or out-push and shove them. You could barely *walk* through that crowd. Some students saw what was happening and tried to protect me. They formed a circle around me but they were no match for gun butts and bayonets. The soldiers got to me, smashed the radio with their gun butts, smashed the camera, and dragged me back behind their lines. I was thrown into the back of a car and taken away somewhere. They kept me overnight and criticized me and took me to the airport the next day. Told me to get out on the next plane.'

Dad went on to say that as soon as they had left him at the airport he took a cab to the foreign hotel compound on the airport road. He figured the Lidu Hotel would be the best place to phone from. He called the Beijing Hotel time and time again, finally getting hold of Eddie, who was all right but worried to death when he got back to the suite to find no one there. Eddie had said to stay at the airport because Dad would never be able to get back to the Beijing Hotel.

'I could hear the gunfire over the phone,' Dad added. 'Eddie said he'd try to find out where you were. It was hell, Alex. All we could do was wait to see if you showed up.'

'What about Eddie?' Mom asked, lighting another cigarette.

Eddie had headed back to the hotel after he had told me he would. He got back safely.

'What happened to his two-way, Dad? He went off the air suddenly and I couldn't raise him again.'

Dad smiled — for the first time a real smile, not a forced one. Eddie had been on his way back to the hotel on the east side of the square. He stopped to look at the students' barricade of buses across the square near the Monument to the Peoples' Heroes. While he was lighting his pipe he dropped the radio.

Over the next few days, I got poked and prodded by the doctor, who said I was 'traumatized' — as if I needed him to tell me that — and clipped and buzzed by a barber — so I am almost blond again with a brushcut.

Xin-hua's videos made it onto the news. There are reports about China on the news almost every night, and the stuff that Xin-hua and I got has been shown — edited, of course — over and over again. It's all there for the world to see.

Eddie sent all my journals and notes over from Beijing, along with a nice letter to Dad and me, saying he was sorry the way things had worked out. He's still there, still at the hotel, still sending reports. He reported that the Chinese government is telling a bag full of lies about what happened in Tian An Men Square on June fourth, just like Xin-hua said they would. They've been rounding up the so-called hooligans and bad elements who caused the so-called counter-revolutionary revolt and executing them. There's a massive hunt on for student leaders and for people who talked to foreign reporters. These people are being shot, too. Eddie found out that after the government shoots someone, they send the victim's family a bill for the bullet.

Last night Dad had to go out after supper. He fussed about leaving me alone – he's barely been out of the house since we got back – but I convinced him I wouldn't fall down in a fit if I was alone for a couple of hours. After he left I flopped in front of the TV, using the remote to flip through the channels, looking for a brainless sitcom to take my mind off things. One of the American channels was showing a program called *Storm in Beijing*.

On the screen was a video clip that had been shot in daylight from the roof of the Beijing Hotel. The date given was June sixth. That would be when I was still at Nai-nai's house. On the screen a convoy of four tanks was rolling down Chang An Avenue towards the hotel, unchallenged in the deserted street. The hatches were closed and the big machine guns up top were covered in canvas.

I felt a chill of fear as the tanks seemed to draw me back to the wide avenue in front of the Forbidden City. My hands shook as I searched for the button on the remote to change the channel.

Suddenly a man sprinted out into the street. He was wearing dark slacks and a white shirt with the sleeves rolled up to his elbows. He carried a little briefcase in one hand, and a rolled-up windbreaker in the other.

He stopped right in front of the lead tank, facing it, defying it, standing almost at attention.

The tank stopped so suddenly the big gun dipped. I held my breath, waiting for the machine-gun burst that would rip the man from his feet and hurl him backwards onto the road. Nothing happened for a moment. Then a belch of diesel smoke spurted from the side of the lead tank. It moved forward, then swung sharply to one side to avoid the man.

The man sidestepped, skipping in a lateral motion that kept him in front of the ugly machine. The tank stopped again. The man stood at attention, challenging. Another belch of smoke as the tank pivoted again, this time to the other side. The man moved with it, forcing it to halt.

Then he walked forward and climbed up onto the tank.

His arm rose and fell as he banged on the hatch. Finally the hatch opened, but no one appeared. The man seemed to be talking to whoever was inside.

He climbed down from the tank and turned his back on it. Again the puff of diesel smoke spurted out the side of the tank. As it began to move forward, the man turned and stood in front of it again, stubborn, unyielding, a thin ordinary man against the military power of the PLA.

Just at that moment, three or four people dressed in civilian clothes ran into the street from the right. They grabbed the man and appeared to plead with him. Finally, they pushed him roughly to the side, his body bent in a bow as he resisted them. The tanks started up again and ground forward along Chang An Avenue, the Avenue of Long Peace.

I let out a sigh, relieved.

On the screen was an American news announcer. He said the man was a student named Wang Ai-min. He had apparently pleaded with the soldiers in the tank to stop the killings that continue in Beijing.

I felt a surge of admiration for the stranger whose name I now knew. He seemed to represent all those people I saw in Tian An Men Square demonstrating for democracy, facing the guns with empty hands. Well, I thought, at least *someone* escaped.

'Shortly after this incident,' the announcer said, 'Wang Ai-min was arrested. Yesterday he was executed.'

I sat there on the couch, numbed by what I had heard. I don't know how long I sat there, probably just a moment or two. But with every passing second something inside me, something like a steel spring, wound tighter and tighter. The TV announcer's words replayed in my head. 'Yesterday he was executed . . . Wang Ai-min was arrested. Yesterday he was executed.' The spring coiled tighter and tighter until it screeched with the tension. 'He was executed . . . executed . . . executed.'

Then the spring snapped.

I jumped up from the couch, screamed something at the top of my voice, and fired the remote against the TV. It hit the top corner, split open, spilling out the batteries, and fell to the floor. I ran from the room, crying and cursing the murderers in uniform who were still murdering, and charged up the stairs and into my room. I stood just inside the door, panting, my wounded leg throbbing from the pounding on the stairs, and glared at the plastic model planes that hung from the ceiling on black threads. I had used black to create the illusion that the planes were actually flying. I punched at the nearest plane, a MIG fighter, and felt a jab of pain as the plane spun on the thread and arced out of reach. I swung again as it arched back towards me and missed. I cursed again and flung open my closet door and rummaged around for a moment before I found an old hockey stick.

Grasping the stick at the blade end I started swinging it like a bat, crying and shouting in anger as I wailed away at the planes. The MIG spun away and cracked into halves against the wall and fell to the floor. A military transport streaked across the room, one wing ripped off it, and plopped onto my bed. It split into bits as I brought the hockey stick down on it. A HUEY helicopter exploded into a thousand pieces that dropped to the floor like plastic rain.

When I had smashed the planes out of the air I turned to the model personnel carrier on my desk. Two quick crushing whacks and it was a small pile of splinters. I turned next to the tanks that guarded my dresser. I imagined a thin isolated figure standing in front of each tank, defiantly. Then I raised the stick over my head. I slammed at the tanks over and over, pounding them into a confusion of dark green plastic bits, bogey wheels, strips of track, and broken guns.

Last came my trophies. They were lined up along a shelf on the wall. I held the stick at arm's length and slid it along the shelf, watching with satisfaction as each trophy toppled off the end of the shelf and crashed to the floor. They lay there in a meaningless pile.

I was still crying, still sobbing, when I stopped. I was breathing heavily. I looked down at my shaking hands. Blood flowed freely from a deep gash in my finger onto the handle of the hockey stick and down to the blade. I threw down the stick and left the room.

I had to walk downstairs carefully. My calf throbbed where the bullet had gone through. I walked into the kitchen and flung open the cupboard where Dad keeps all the pots. I yanked out the biggest, a Corning glass saucepan, sending the rest of the pots crashing down and tumbling out onto the floor. Holding the pot, I went down into the basement, switching on the light when I got to the bottom of the stairs.

The ancient Xi'an army stood silently – the honour guard of the First Emperor – in formation. The bowmen were kneeling, their empty hands waiting for the arrows that I hadn't made yet, the long arrows that they would hold in a formal pose. In my head I heard Lao Xu's quiet voice. 'Thank you for lending us your arrows, Cao Cao. You can be sure we will return them soon!' The overhead light gleamed on the soldiers' bright clothing and winked on the brass coloured studs on their armour. Six men remained to be painted.

I limped to the hot plate I use for making the soldiers, slammed the pot onto it, and turned the control knob to MEDIUM. I hobbled over to the big cupboard, pulled open the doors, and began to lift out the shoe boxes inside. I placed them on the Xi'an display board and unpacked the lead soldiers from the cotton batting inside, standing them upright on the painted plywood. Then I tossed the shoe boxes and cotton aside.

I stepped over to the hot plate and turned the heat to HIGH. In a few moments the bottom of the pot glowed cherry red. I went to the Xi'an display and gathered up a handful of the new two-thousand-year-old lead soldiers. The blood from my finger leaked onto their armour.

I carried them to the hot plate and dropped them into th
pot.

The paint smoked and burned as the soldiers began to melt.
limped to the table, scooped up more soldiers, fed them into th
pot one by one. The bottom of the pot was a lake of lead and eacl
bloodied soldier sank slowly into it.

I worked steadily, calmly. When the Xi'an army was gone
began on the others, lifting them to the pot, dropping them in on
after the other, Horsemen of the Light Brigade, guerrilla fighter
from Dien Bien Phu, Canadian infantry from Vimy Ridge
Mounties and Metis from Frog Lake, bows, arrows, cannon
sabres, rifles, machine guns. All the soldiers from all the war
melted down together into lead again.

Later on, Dad came home. From my room I heard him come in
slam the door, utter an exclamation. Footsteps raced to th
basement door, clattered down the stairs, creaked slowly u
again.

In the kitchen, the sounds of tea being made – water running
the whistle of the kettle, the clink of spoons in mugs. Then Dad'
footsteps climbing the stairs to my room. Silently he handed me
mug of tea and sat at the foot of the bed, holding his tea in botl
hands. He sat there, silent, for a few moments.

'You know, Alex, I think I've finally started to grow up.'

I leaned back against the headboard and said nothing, jus
waited.

'Even when the soldiers roared into the square and jumpe
down from the trucks I was still at it, still trying to get the perfec
image, you know? Still after the great award-winning shot. A
if I wasn't there, as if I was a camera, not a person, not . .
involved.'

He shook his head and took a sip of his tea. I looked into hi
face. He was confused. This was hard for him. He was trying t
work things out, like Xin-hua when she explained about the PL
in the Five Pagoda Temple compound.

'Even when I was being arrested, part of me was saying, This is great! The big newsman arrested while he tried to get the story out to the public. Hero stuff.

Then when I realized that you weren't at the hotel, that you were *gone*, it wasn't a game anymore.'

He stopped talking and swallowed hard. His hand trembled as he raised the mug to his lips and sipped the steaming tea.

'I realized it could have been *you* Alex. All those kids about your age, shot down, bleeding in the street. Any one of them could have been you.'

Dad looked around the room, composing himself again. His eyes rested on my dresser, then my desk. The tank and armoured personnel carrier models had been beaten into bits. He looked up at the empty strings dangling from my ceiling. He nodded slowly.

'So it's all gone,' he murmured.

'Pardon, Dad?'

'All that work you put in, Alex. All those hours. And the lead soldiers, they're gone too.'

Then I knew what he meant. 'I guess it was all a game to me too, Dad,' I said. 'It isn't anymore.'

I thought about Beijing, the big spring winds, the walls and alleys, the Forbidden City and Tian An Men Square. The night filled with machine-gun fire and screams, crackling flames and Lao Xu's shout of outrage before he died. And, a few days later, that single crack of gunfire.

I hadn't been able to do anything to help. I hadn't been able to stop anything.

I had known two real heroes in my life and they were both dead. I had seen another on TV today and he was dead, too. Not one of them had worn a uniform.

I took a long drink of my warm tea. 'Nothing will be the same now, will it, Dad? Everything will be different, and we will too.'

A couple of moments passed before he answered.

'Yeah, but we can't let this get us down. We can't let this beat us.' Dad's voice had some of the old fire in it. His eyes sparkled. He tried to smile. 'Right, Shanty?'

I smiled too and shook my head. 'It's Shan Da, Dad.'

Afterword

The number of those killed in the Beijing massacre on June 4, 1989 has never been offically recorded.

Approximately one month after the incident, Chen Xi-tong, Mayor of Beijing, submitted his report to the Politburo of the Communist Party of China. 'During the whole operation,' he wrote, 'no one, including those who refused but were forced to leave, died.'

A Note on the Pronunciation of Chinese names:

The Chinese names in this book are given in the official form of transcription called Pin Yin, and each syllable is given separately. Here is a brief pronunciation guide for surnames:

Xu – *Hssoo*
Wang – *Wong*
Nie – *Nee-uh*
Liu – *Lee-oh*
Zhao – *Jow* to rhyme with the bow of a boat

Other words:

Lao – pronounce the "A" as in *father*
Xiao – long "I" and long "A": *hss-e-a-oh*

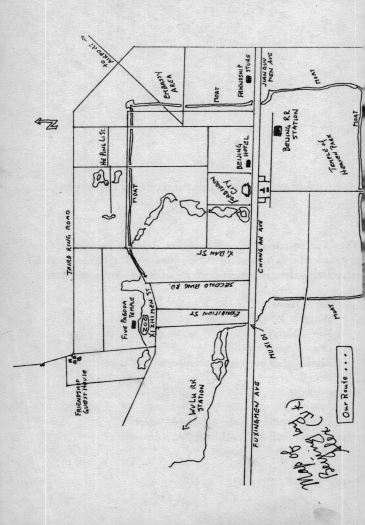

Map (in part) of
Beijing (北京)

To Airport →

Embassy Area

Third Ring Road

He Ping Li St.

MOAT

Friendship Store

Jian Guo Men Ave

MOAT

Beijing Hotel

Beijing RR Station

Temple of Heaven Park

MOAT

Forbidden City

Xi Dan St.

Chang An Ave

Five Pagoda Temple

ZOO

Xizhimen St.

Second Ring Rd.

Exhibition St.

Muxioi

Fuxingmen Ave

Friendship Guest House

Wulu RR Station

Our Route · · · ·